T0064568

DEPRIVATIONAL
MEAN

DEPRIVATIONAL MEAN

Fortune Freeze

CORY PERALA

authorHOUSE®

AuthorHouse™ LLC
1663 Liberty Drive
Bloomington, IN 47403
www.authorhouse.com
Phone: 1-800-839-8640

Published by AuthorHouse   08/22/2013

ISBN: 978-1-4918-0919-8 (sc)
ISBN: 978-1-4918-0918-1 (e)

Library of Congress Control Number: 2013914773

CONTENTS

CHAPTER 1

"Roy, have you ever thought of taking your coffee shops international with franchises in Europe and Asia?" says a news reporter standing in front of Roy Monte at a press conference.

"I have thought about that option, I find the five Don's Coffee Shops are enough to handle at this moment," says Roy.

Roy is wearing a flannel dress shirt and tie, brown hair cowlick slanting to the left reaching down to his left temple. His tall frame is too tall for the podium he stands behind. The nice gold Rolex on his right wrist is large enough to be used as a club.

"May I ask, where 'Don' comes from in your business name?" says a different reporter standing among the group of reporters.

"Yes, Don comes from the first name of my favorite school teacher in middle school. He was the most inspirational teacher I had," says Roy.

"Mr. Monte, are you ready for your climb up Mt. McKinley later this month?" says the same news reporter after writing on a note pad from the previous response.

"I can't wait to be put to the test by McKinley. I'm ready, I've been training for it over a year now," says Roy.

"What is your vision about the new Travel Lodge Hotel just recently opening for business here in town?" says a journalist while raising his hand and a pencil tucked in his ear.

"The Travel Lodge will be a place of opportunity, relaxation, and fun. I can't wait to see the positive impact it will have on the Trenton community. With hotels being booked here all the time, the demand for another hotel is much needed," says Roy.

A short journalist wearing a navy blue shirt in the back row waves his arm frantically to be recognized by Roy.

"Here we go last question, yes, to you in the navy blue shirt," says Roy with a surprising look.

"Sir, your business model has recently been in Business Week Magazine, what makes your model different from everyone else?" says the journalist in the back.

"The difference being mind set I used to acquire the capital necessary to start the businesses I have today. You see, I don't read books, I write them. I don't look forward to buying a new house; I look forward to buying an apartment building to rent to others. I don't buy products; I buy companies that make the products. Thank you and have a good day," says Roy.

Roy leaves the podium area to go to his next scheduled event of the day. The group of reporters continues to take pictures and write down notes of Roy as he leaves the podium and walks into an adjacent side room.

"Hooah! Buddy Casey, can you move a mountain?" says Roy with open arms while walking out of the press room.

"Yes, I can move a mountain Roy, do you believe I can do it?" says Casey with his big head of long blond hair just enough to cover his ears. Casey has a big muscular build body about double the size of Roy wearing kaki pants and a red polo shirt.

"I'm a believer you can move a mountain, can you climb a mountain?" says Roy.

"The only thing stopping me is my self," says Casey.

"Hooah! It's often the response to adversity that determines a person's probability of success," says Roy walking along side Casey one step ahead.

Roy and Casey face each other and complete a secret hand shake, alternating pounding fists on top of one another, alternating a low five slap on top of one another, and ending with a high five.

"I heard you were going to climb Mt. McKinley soon, is it alright if I come with Roy?" says Casey.

"It will be just like old times when we were deliverers at Chester's Chicken," says Roy.

"Except, this time I get to pull my own weight," says Casey.

"You better be pulling your own weight, I'm not carrying your ass up McKinley on foot," says Roy.

"Don't worry, I've been hitting the gym with two-a-days for the past six months," says Casey bending both elbows out to his side and flexing his biceps to make his biceps double in size.

"We leave Thursday, let me know when you can be there for the plane leaving at ten in the morning," says Roy.

"Climb on! By the way Roy, how many times does it take to succeed?" says Casey with enthusiasm.

CHAPTER 2

The face mask has no use in trying to stop the penetration of the cold mountain air hitting Roy's face. The only material to truly absorb the mountain air is a persons own body nothing can stop it. At 9,000 feet, Roy and Casey have a rope connected to each others waist and walking side ways across the mountain to get a better angle towards the peak.

"Casey, once we get to that peninsula where the mountain bows out, the degree of incline will be less and make an easier climb," says Roy pointing to the peninsula ahead and looking back at Casey.

The cloudy day casts a dark shadow in the inlet of the mountain peninsula. Snow gets kicked up by the strong wind in the inlet and blows the snow upward in a circular motion. The peninsula teases the two climbers due to their current position on the mountain having a difficult incline.

"Roy, there's no one to tell us what to do up here. What a get away, I think I might just move in," says Casey stopping to catch his breath.

Roy stops too and says, "I'm sure your wife and kids will feel the same way. In fact, we think alike."

"I know you have sacrificed a lot with your business ventures and choosing a career over family. There is nothing wrong with that Roy. If that's what you are going to do with your life, promise me one thing. Promise me that you will see it through to the end, and not stopping when your businesses become a success," says Casey lightly covered with powdered snow.

"I promise my intentions are to stay active creating action goals. I find it's the doing that makes me the most happy, not the numbers of profit or expense ratio," says Roy looking down at his foot in the snow trail leading to Casey.

Suddenly there is a loud crackling sound from above. The snow starts to move and the wind slows down for a brief moment and then picks up speed again.

"What was that?" says Casey.

"Both climbers pause and stare as a massive snow bank gives way directly above them creating an avalanche. The wave of snow picks up speed and becomes bigger as it approaches.

"Oh my god! Oh lord!" says Casey.

Roy pulls out his radio to try call for help, "Help! Help! There is an avalanche on the east side of the mountain, come in, over."

"Roy, lets stay together, here, grab my harness," says Casey unclipping the rope attaching Roy to him and running to Roy grabbing his harness.

The blast of snow engulfs the two climbers with a massive force that pushes them apart down the mountain side, engulfing them both in snow as they continue to move downward with the land slide.

*   *   *

"McKinley Mountain Unit 29 can you read me? McKinley Mountain Unit 29 do you come in? Over!"

Susan occupied with reporting the day's weather is caught up from the noise of the incoming radio signal. Drastically grabbing for the radio responding, "Mountain Unit 29 here, this is Susan. What is the problem?"

Susan wears her green mountain ranger uniform with a Mountain Unit 29 gold patch on her left chest. She has long red hair and small lens glasses. She shifts her pear shaped body forward as she waits for a responding message.

"This is Roy Monte, there has been an avalanche on the north side of McKinley Mountain; my partner Casey is no where to be seen, and I took a fall in a nearby cave when the avalanche came through, and—hhhrrr—and broke my left leg," says Roy stopping to gasp for breath.

Susan making eye contact with ranger Gilbert sitting behind his desk across the room shows a surprising look on her face.

Susan replies back, "We will be sending out a rescue team as soon as possible, so hang tight. Do you know your approximate elevation?"

Roy applying a hoarse voice from the pain that he is in says, "Elevation around 10,000 feet, please hurry."

Gilbert looks at Susan showing a clear reflection of light off his bald head says, "I'll tell the others."

Just then, the radio communication between the Mountain Unit and Roy is lost. Gilbert walks across to the room's entrance in a slow stride and opens the door sending a wave of cold air into the room. Once outside, he goes across the drive way into the equipment shop where

Ron and Jack are fixing machinery. Sam is blasting away with the tunes of Led Zeppelin with her hair up in a pony tail wearing a white tank top that is too big for her skinny upper body.

The thick beard and eyebrows of Gilbert make his head seem bigger than it actually is. His mountain ranger apparel is one size too small for him, so his pant legs extend down to above his ankles to show his boot lacings. Sam notices Gilbert enter. She rubs her neck to show her black scorpion tattoo on the side of her neck. Jack and Ron have noticed Gilbert enter too and both are kneeling on the ground. Jack's black hair, big nose, and broad shoulders make him identical to Paul Bunyan. Ron has on a red Harley Davidson shirt, which matches his Irish features. He has a partial bald head of red hair and side burns.

Gilbert interrupts and says, "Listen up; we have a mission to accomplish. There are two climbers stranded from an avalanche on the mountain; Sam ready the chopper."

*   *   *

Within a half hour the four are in the chopper heading to the East side of Mt. McKinley because that is the closest landing to Roy and Casey's location. Gilbert sitting in the passenger seat in the cockpit of the chopper turns around and tells Susan in the back. "The East side landing looks too steep to land the helicopter so we will have to try for Carol's Plateau on the West side of the mountain."

Seconds after saying that, the helicopter shakes rapidly from a gust of wind. Then Jack asks Susan with a curious look on his face. "What is the weather looking like?" Susan sits behind her laptop clearing her long hair from her face looks with fright in her eyes. Her hand shakes while she keys in on the laptop.

"Let's do it," says Sam with a pleasing look on her face while retightening her wrist watches on both wrists.

Susan says "We are in for a ride gang the weather has taken a turn for the worse. The winds are at 50 mph and expected to get blizzard like conditions."

As they descend on to Carol's Plateau the chopper shakes and makes a whirl wind of snow around them making visibility poor. As Jack opens the door of the helicopter the noise from it becomes deafening to the ears. As they get all the luggage out of the chopper, Susan screams at the top of her lungs. "Let's get moving gang before the weather gets any worse."

As they begin walking toward the north side of the mountain, the helicopter gradually gets up to speed and leaves. The landing gear emerges out of the snow from being submerged one foot deep. The whirl wind of snow and ice gets bigger and vanishes into the air. The unit moves out in a single filed line. Jack eventually hollers at Sam, "Quit doodling around and keep up with the group. What? Didn't you eat your Wheaties this morning?"

Sam quickly replies back, "I am just looking at the scenery so stop nagging at me."

As they keep walking the wind and the snow accumulates a sheet of ice on their masks and jackets. Gradually, Susan hears Gilbert complain about his two cut off fingers; they don't have any circulation through them and are cold. After the fourth hour on the mountain they stop for water.

Gilbert says, "It looks like we have a straight climb up about three hundred feet so get your picks and rope out to ready your harness."

As they get half way up the cliff the conditions worsen; the snow fall is thick making the visibility and climbing worse. The four climbers are harnessed together each in file about five feet below one another. Then Jack's pick slips out of the rock and falls past Sam who is just below him. Jack falls freely about ten feet when his safety harness catches with the climbing rope jolting him to a standstill. Additional weight is now put on the rest of the climbers because they are holding Jack's weight.

Susan yells, "Gilbert, I'm giving way; can't hold." Her legs work drastically as her spiked boots gain back footing into the mountains cliff. Jack comes back to his senses and drives his pick into the nearest rock. He then gains control and resumes climbing to the top; relieving the tension from the other climbers safety harness.

"You okay?" Sam says with concern to Jack.

"Yeah, I was born okay. Sorry everyone, I'm better than that, it won't happen again," Jack says.

Susan says, "Be careful here we can not afford to loose any time." The unit reaches the top of the cliff exhausted; there legs are strained and feel like rubber.

Susan grabs for her radio and signals for Roy over the radio. "Roy do you read me; Roy do you copy?"

Roy mumbles "I copy, where are you guys?"

Susan coming up with an idea to find where Roy says, "Roy do you have a GPS; if you do what is your coordinates?"

"My position is 61 degrees latitude with—150 degrees longitude," says Roy.

Susan looks at her GPS screen and sees that they're only 200 feet away. She moves her eyes left to right in deep thought as if reading from her cognitive memory. The solution of how to get there comes to her gradually building momentum, slowly processing the problem to find the solution.

"Just a little ways to go," says Susan to the others.

Gilbert unbuckles his back pack sending it plummeting into the foot of snow beneath the surface. He readies the collapsible sled to put Roy into. The team follows Susan as she tries to find the exact coordinates on her GPS.

They stop hiking with Susan saying, "Well, this is the spot."

Sam looks around and says "What do you mean? There is no cave here!"

"It's covered with snow; carefully use your picks," Gilbert says while equipping his hands with picks and lowering himself on all fours.

He begins to poke around into the snow surface trying to find the loosely covered opening. The others do the same. They continue to drive their picks looking as if they were trying to find a needle in a hay stack because of the unreasonable amount of time this is taking. Sam's pick sinks into the snow and then she crawls ahead another two feet: this time the pick falls in with a chunk of snow falling freely; having Sam's hand fall over the side of the caves edge. This small opening that is revealed begins to take in a rush of outside air. The remaining layer of snow over the opening weakens and gives away its strength. The rest of the opening is noticeable being about four feet wide.

"Hey guys over here!" Sam yells for the others.

Gilbert gets to his back pack and the sled by running as if he has sand bags tied to his feet while he progresses slowly through the snow. The members meet at Sam's location.

Jack yells down into the cave, "Roy! Roy, are you there?" The cave echoes his voice; bouncing it around the rocky side walls.

"Yes, right here," says Roy while waving his right arm back and forth making himself faintly visible for the climbers to see him forty feet down.

The climbers ready the climbing rope with Sam, Susan, and Gilbert backing away from the edge to keep tension on the rope as the big man Jack does the heavy lifting.

Jack yells down at Roy, "Roy we are sending down some rope; tie it around your mid-section we'll pull you up." Jack tosses the rope down; as it falls to the floor the rope starts in a folded circular form and unwinds in a spiraling motion until impact. Roy has to reposition himself and scoots backwards making his upper body do all the work so he can reach the rope. With each slide he squints his eyes and grunts, "hahh . . . hahh!"

When he reaches the rope it takes him more than one try to tie the knot; he can not feel his hands from the cold. After struggling, the knot is tied; he tugs on the rope a couple of times signaling for the hoist. Jack begins hoisting by first bending his knees low and back straight pulling upward as he grips for additional line. The action has the lower body moving first and transferring energy up through his arms in an upright row.

The others are amazed at Jacks strength and how easy he is making it look. One arms pull of the rope for Jack is equal to two pulls for the typical human being. Jacks footing begins to shake as the cave's edge starts to give way with falling snow chunks at the edge.

"How does he get the strength?" says Sam.

"It's more than just that, its courage and sacrifice to help others; and if it comes to it, putting yourself in harms way," says Gilbert while taking the slack out of the rope line leading to Jack.

Jack starts to breathe heavily half way in the hoisting. Roy's image emerges as he comes closer to the surface with falling pieces of snow around him.

Jack starts to lose his breath becoming tired. Five feet away from the surface Jack mumbles, "HHrr! Come on a little more!"

Gilbert standing with the others holding Roy's weight says, "Sam go help pull Roy up and out."

Sam trudges through the snow to the caves edge and puts out his hand for the emerging Roy to grab on to. Roy reaches up and grabs Sam's hand. The grab makes a firm connection. Jack then bends down to grab his other arm. The two simultaneously pull him out with their strength. Roy lands face first into the surface. Roy lies there motionless leaving Sam and Jack sitting next to him breathing heavily and exhausted. Gilbert and Susan bring up the supplies and carefully slide Roy onto the snow sled. The repositioning of Roy's body causes his broken leg to shift.

"Hhaa!" Roy yells.

Susan opens a canteen feeding water into Roy's mouth. Gilbert tends to the broken leg by splinting it into the normal position.

"Have you found Casey?" Roy asks.

"No, we haven't looked yet; right now we got to get you out of here," Gilbert says.

"We can go back to Carol's Plateau to air lift him out of here, and get more supplies," says Sam who is finally recovered and standing from trying to pull Roy up.

"It is unlikely that Casey is alive yet. He's been probably buried in the snow for half a day now," says Jack who has finally caught up with his breathing.

"What ever the case is he is not going to be left on this mountain." says Sam.

*　　*　　*

Twenty-four hours later, Roy is back recovering in a hospital bed at nearby Anchorage, Alaska. With a broken leg and severe frost bite on his hands and feet, an IV pole and EKG is monitoring his body fluids and heart beat. The warm beam of sunlight hits Roy's face as he lies in a motionless state.

Sam enters with her wearing a black tank top, snow pants, and black hair up in a pony tail.

"Hey Roy, ready to climb McKinley again?" says Sam with a smile.

"Did you find Casey?" says Roy.

"We are still looking, if there is no sign of his existence in the next eighteen hours, the search will be called off. No one can survive in that kind of temperature for more than three days," says Sam.

"I should have died on that mountain, not him. If only I went along with his advice to head east from Carol's plateau, we would not have had this happen to us," says Roy.

Sitting down in a rocking chair next to Roy's bed, Sam leans forward and places her left hand over her mouth. She opens her mouth to say something, but is stopped by Roy before she can talk.

"I do not regret attempting to climb Mt. McKinley. Now I can say I gave it a shot. Were you going to say something Sam?" says Roy.

"Keep your head up, we have no control over what occurs only what we do when it does occur. Just keep trying and trying. How many times does it take to succeed?" says Sam interlocking her finger tips together beneath her chin.

CHAPTER 3

Nearly a year later Roy is back in Trenton, Minnesota vigorously managing his coffee shops and hotel. Using a cane to get around, his broken leg is expected to heal fully with good recovery. At his apartment, Roy sits at his office desk/kitchen table. This is the start of a busy Monday forecasting a break even analysis and tallying up employee pay roll.

Roy's cell phone rings at his desk, interfering with his concentration. He knocks his knuckles against his temple repeatedly and closes the note book he is writing in. Sitting back in the chair, Roy looks up at the ceiling vent and sighs with relief.

Answering the call, "Hi, this is Roy," says Roy.

"Roy, my name is Todd with Channel 8 News and I would like to do a short interview about your experiences at Mt. McKinley. Are you able to take a few minutes to answer a few of my questions?" says Todd with an enthusiastic voice.

"Yes, I can give you a few minutes," says Roy sitting back in his black leather office chair and minimizing his computer screen with a focused expression.

"First of all, tell me a little about your recovery after returning to Trenton," says Todd.

"My left leg has not fully healed yet, so I use a cane to walk around where ever I go. The blood flow in my hands and feet is limited due to the frost bite that I experienced," says Roy pausing.

"Has anyone approached you about the mental aspects of the recovery, if so, what are they?" says Todd.

"Eleven months ago, I had a person tell me that they were surprised to see that I was still alive. Four months ago, I had someone tell me that I would never be able to fully recover from my injuries and to keep faith. Today, I'm back at my life's work holding a fortune in palm of my hand. I know at any given moment it can be taken away from me," says Roy.

"What do you mean it can be taken away from you?" says Todd.

"My assets are being taxed at an ever increasing rate with nearly a third of my income being part of it. I understand that wealth creation should benefit everyone, but this also makes me want to work less for my pursuit of happiness," says Roy swiveling his chair in a circle.

"Interesting, back to the mountain experience, what was going through your mind while being trapped in that mountain avalanche?" says Todd.

"All I could think about is my safety and just trying to breathe. I was so cold, in pain, and numb at the same time. The thought of my life back in Trenton kept me going," says Roy.

"Great, that is all I need today. Is it okay if I release the contents of this interview to the public?" says Todd.

"Fine by me," says Roy.

"Have a good day Roy," says Todd.

"Bye Todd," says Roy hanging up the phone, frozen in place to reflect on what he just said.

Roy looks at the clock on the kitchen stove and sees that it is exactly twelve noon. Staring long at the clock it changes eventually to twelve o' one, Roy has pleasing look on his face. Then at twelve o' two, Roy has a disgruntled look at the clock. Finally, at twelve o' three his eyes widen to look frantically around in the pursuit of something. Getting up, Roy searches through his phone book and dials a number on his cell phone.

"Yes, I'm calling for a Dr. Hasert, is he available?" says Roy.

Waiting, Roy writes on a piece of paper a name and showing a wide eyed expression.

"Yes, Dr. Hasert my name is Roy Monte and I would like to schedule a consultation with you about cryogenic freezing," says Roy.

Pausing, Roy looks over his schedule.

"Tomorrow at two works great, see you then," says Roy ending the conversation.

*   *   *

At a local sports bar, Roy sits at a dinner table with Shannon a good business colleague of his over the years. Shannon has black hair down to her shoulders and finely trimmed eyebrows. Much of her dark green clothing blends in with the darkness of dim lighting.

"So where do you think you will be in ten years Roy? You are not married, not currently dating, and you're a hard working entrepreneur," says Shannon.

"I like to think that I will not be here, I want my heart to be beating but not be here," says Roy with palms up just above the table and a head tilt up and back.

"Odd, what do you mean?" says Shannon with a confusing look and fidgeting with her silver necklace.

Roy points to the T.V. screen showing the local news reporting a news topic on Roy Monte.

"Please turn that up," Shannon shouts to one of the waiters.

"Roy Monte, the owner of Don's Coffee Shop and Travel Lodge Hotel, will be in federal court tomorrow to seek authority to be cryogenically frozen for fifty years. This will keep his assets growing by being still alive, which he believes will benefit everyone," says the news anchor on the T.V.

Switching to a TV shot of Roy in an interview, "Technically, I will still be alive since Dr. Hasert has discovered a way to bring cells back to life after the cryogenics process is complete. While frozen, my stock holdings and businesses will continue to grow creating more wealth generation. I feel the court should really pass this law for the benefits my wealth will have for everyone," says Roy on the T.V. screen.

"Roy, what are you doing? Fifty years from now you will not recognize anyone," says Shannon.

"I'm looking forward to it," says Roy.

"Don't you want to be with your friends, your generation that you grew up in?" says Shannon.

"I will still have memories and memories are all that I have right now any way," says Roy showing less emotion with not wanting to prove a point for being cryogenically frozen.

*   *   *

At the court house, the court room is full with reporters waiting outside for day one of the hearing. The court room has all varnished wooden furniture and walls with white ceramic tile. The judge motions to begin the court process.

"Roy Monte, we are here today for a decision on the legality and righteousness of intentional cryogenic freezing. Cryogenics is an emerging discovery that is not for certain with unknown risks," says judge Flemming being a woman of curly hair, bright red lipstick, and wearing a black gown.

"I'm aware of those risks your honor. It is a procedure that is possible and has been done in mammals. From a medical standpoint, what is the difference between a risky separation of Siamese twins and my cryogenic proposal? The Siamese twins are separated for a better life. Me, I choose to be frozen to grow my business and grow my assets. This will allow me to help others and fulfill my pursuit of happiness," says Roy.

"The question with righteousness of cryogenics is who is at fault if a cryogenically frozen person does not live the process?" says Flemming with a high set of eye brows to show her mascara and eyes looking over to the jury.

The prosecution and defense give their opening statements to the court. The prosecution claims their proposed cryogenics freezing is in the pursuit of happiness, then the defense gives their explanation of cryogenic freezing in pursuing wealth is an irrelevant reason. The prosecution goes first with a scholarly historian explaining the true of pursuing happiness from America's founding fathers.

Pausing, the court room is silently waiting for the defense being the U.S. Health Care Association. A tall brown hair woman in a white suit is sitting next to the defense lawyer in gray suit with tie, black hair, and a double chin.

"The defense calls Craig Jones, Health Law Advisor for the U.S. Health Care Committee to the stand," says defense lawyer Kinelt.

"As you wish Kinelt," says Flemming to defense lawyer Harry Kinelt.

Walking up to the stand next to Craig Jones, Kinelt faces the jury while asking his first question. Craig's short buzz cut hair makes his skull protrude and show itself. He wears a dark blue dress shirt with a black tie and black pants.

"The biggest question to solve in this case is going to be, is cryogenics right or wrong? Based on this, are there any infringements with conducting cryogenics to any laws in healthcare?" says Kinelt to Jones.

"Yes, there is no standardized procedure written to date on conducting cryogenics, which is required for every procedure in health care. Cryogenics is also a procedure needing equipment not invented yet. Not only that, but financial brokers do not have policies and options for people freezing themselves and keeping there financial assets still alive," says Jones.

"If Roy Monte were to become cryogenically frozen, what would be his likelihood for survival?" says Kinelt.

"I would say fifty percent death and fifty percent survival," says Jones grabbing his neck tie with both hands to tighten it.

"That is all your honor," says Kinelt bowing to judge Flemming with hands clasped behind his back.

"Along with risk, what aspect of cryogenics makes it so dangerous?" says Flemming to Jones.

"Cryogenics is dangerous due to the water in the blood expanding when frozen. This can rupture blood vessels or veins in the heart and brain, leading to severe if not fatal internal bleeding. If this cryogenics procedure is to be tried at all, the unthawing of the body will have to be very slow," says Jones.

With the opportunity to question Jones, it's the prosecution lawyer's turn. Lisa questions Jones while walking towards him. She wears a light blue dress top and skirt with brown hair and brown eyes.

"In health care, what is the ideal indicator that a person is pronounced dead? How does it tie into the cryogenic procedure?" says Lisa.

"The heart rate is the biggest indicator of when a person is considered living. With the cryogenics process, the heart does not have a heart rate due to the effects of freezing," says Jones.

"Now, with open heart surgeries, does the heart stop beating for even a few minutes while being hooked up to a machine for a number of minutes?" says Lisa pacing back and forth across the court room.

"Yes, there are procedures of this kind done all the time," says Jones.

"Having the heart stop beating during open heart surgery in many aspects then is similar to the proposed cryogenic procedure in this case. Is it not?" says Lisa.

"Yes, they are similar in those aspects, the only difference is the blood is not frozen, it is simply cooled. The duration of time with no heart beat is also a significant indicator," says Jones.

"The differences between cooling the blood to just above freezing and cooling it to below freezing, what are they? Is it possible to cool the blood above freezing and freeze the rest of the body?" says Lisa.

"The blood cells would decompose if not frozen, making reviving the patient almost impossible after fifty years," says Jones.

"No further questions your honor," says Lisa not getting a favorable professional opinion from Jones.

*   *   *

Day two of the U.S Health Care Committee vs. Roy Monte case looks to finalize the decision about the upcoming future of cryogenics. Rising out of her chair is Roy's lawyer, Lisa. Lisa motions for a Health Care Economic Advisor by the name of Wanu Chen to the stand. Wanu is very thin woman in her late thirties wearing a red sweater and over a white t-shirt.

"Wanu, what impact can cryogenics have on business in the health care industry?" says Lisa.

"The emergence of cryogenics in the health care industry can have the potential to raise the country's gross income five percent. This would produce more jobs for conducting the procedure and manufacturing the equipment needed," says Wanu.

After the hour long court process, the jury leaves to vote the decision of the case.

Twenty minutes later, judge Flemming and members of the jury enter the silent court room waiting for the decision.

"Roy Monte, please rise for the results of the jury," says Flemming. "Voting unanimously fifteen to two, the jury approves the right to allow cryogenics for individuals in the Unites States of America. This court is adjourned." Flemming hits the hammer and gavel.

Roy's look of relief closes his eyes with Lisa smiling and shaking hands with Roy to congratulate him.

Walking out of the court house, Roy is almost run over at the door steps by reporters.

"What will you do the day before being cryogenically frozen?' says a reporter.

"When will you conduct the procedure? Who will do the procedure?" says a journalist.

"Do you think congress will want to consider the case? Will congress step in and convene?" says the journalist wearing a black baseball cap on backwards and pencil tucked in his right ear.

Saying nothing to answer the swarming questions around him, Roy walks through the journalists and reporters. He quickly gets into the back seat of a taxi waiting for him.

"401 43rd street," says Roy to the cab driver after buckling his seat belt.

"You won the case huh, how many times does it take to succeed?" says the cab driver wearing a Chicago Cubs baseball cap.

"Obviously you do not know, the Chicago Cubs haven't won a world series in over a hundred years," says Roy.

"One hundred? Hey, enough of that can we please change the topic?" says the cab driver straightening his hat.

CHAPTER 4

"Dr. Menzel here," says the thirty-five year old, five foot eight, blond hair Dr. Menzel on the phone.

"Yes, my name is Roy Monte, the reason I'm calling today is for the opportunity to conduct the first cryogenics on me. Now, I will conduct an agreement in writing and a five hundred thousand dollar sign on bonus to get things under way," says Roy.

"Yes, I'm listening and very interested to see what I can do for you Mr. Monte," says Menzel in an enthusiastic tone of voice.

"I will stop by your office tomorrow over the lunch hour, does that work?" says Roy.

"Yes, any way to accommodate you Mr. Monte," says Dr. Menzel with a face of bewilderment from not knowing where to conduct the consultation.

The next day, Roy meets Dr. Menzel in his office at the Trenton Hospital. Seeing Dr. Menzel waiting at his desk, he wears a white button up long sleeve shirt and neck tie underneath. Roy sits down with his leather binder in a chair in front of the desk. A tropical plant sitting on the floor to right side of the desk is just beginning to bloom.

The flowers head is the shape of a square, orange, and peppered with black dots.

"Before we get started, I have one question, if I should die during the fifty year period of the cryogenics freeze, how will I be compensated?" says Dr. Menzel.

"Compensation will be given each quarter you are overlooking my cryogenics. I will have an attorney assigned to overlook the process and payment structure based on rules I have established. A medical lawyer named, Julia will also be working with you on my behalf," says Roy.

"When do you plan to start the cryogenics procedure?" says Dr. Menzel already sounding interested in conditions of the operation.

"ASAP, I'm waiting to hear back from Trinex about their completion of the cryogenic housing chamber and software program to run it. They gave me an estimation of about three weeks to completion," says Roy acting as if that is not soon enough by lifting his hand off one knee with palm up.

"I will need to learn how to run the equipment as well as run a trial test," says Dr. Menzel.

"Well, we don't have a moment to lose now do we? A Trinex Representative will stop by one week from today at the same time to inform you of everything you need to know," says Roy.

"Okay," says Dr. Menzel looking at his schedule for next week and being confused about how he is going to fit in the appointment.

Roy hands over agreement papers of the procedure to Dr. Menzel to be signed. The papers consist of five pages with Roy's signature already on them. Dr. Menzel takes out a black marble pen from his pants pocket, twists it and begins reading through the forms.

Dr. Menzel reads every word and signs the papers a few minutes later. His pager goes off, signaling he is needed to help a patient. He looks at his waist to read the pager on his right side by pulling his white lab jacket out of the way.

"I have to get going Roy, I'm needed in the Intensive Care Unit," says Dr. Menzel standing up out of his chair quickly.

"Are you left handed?" says Roy.

"I'm right handed," says Dr. Menzel.

"You will need some creativity to make this procedure happen. Use the right side of your brain, your creative side. The next time you see me, will be at the procedure," says Roy.

"I will do my best Roy, pardon me I must be dismissed," says Dr. Menzel leaving his office walking around the left side of the desk.

Grabbing the completed paperwork with all the legal documents of the procedure, Roy puts them in his leather binder and leaves the office room after Dr. Menzel.

*   *   *

As Roy lies on a medical operating table, an EKG monitor and IV is hooked to him. Two bright operating lights shine down on Roy with Dr. Menzel being the only person in the room.

"Okay Roy, we are going to lift you into the cryogenics freezing chamber, which is at zero degrees Fahrenheit," says Dr. Menzel with his surgical mask muffling his voice.

Four people enter the room wearing blue scrubs and lift Roy up, separating the table platform from the surgery bed frame below. The table platform is made for the deep freeze chamber by locking into the bottom. With a see through glass door and key pad lock, the chamber is made of stainless steel.

"What are you looking forward to seeing in fifty years Roy?" says Dr. Menzel in a white surgery suit, blue hair net, and purple rubber gloves on his hands.

"I'm looking forward to my enormous fortune," says Roy getting sleepy from the anesthetics being administered.

"I'm about to begin the deep freeze solution that will cool your blood. How many times does it take to succeed Roy?" says Dr. Menzel's Assistant attaching the deep freeze solution bag to the IV.

The bright light shining down on Roy is the last visual sense Roy experiences as his vision blurs. His body slowly relaxes and his mouth drops loosely open and his eyes close.

CHAPTER 5

"Roy, Roy can you hear me Roy?" says a familiar face looking Roy in the eyes.

"Oh, yep I hear you," says Roy as if he has lost his voice and blinking his eyes rapidly.

Lifting his right arm, Roy makes a fist toward the ceiling and opens his hand to spread his fingers out. Roy sits up from the bed he is in shivering from the cold temperatures.

"You did it; the shivering should go away in about an hour because your body temperature is trying to find its homeostasis. I'm Dr. Menzel by the way," says Dr. Menzel.

"Dr. Menzel, you're still alive! I recognize you. How many years has it been?" says Roy.

"It's been fifty years and the year is 2074," says Dr. Menzel.

"Ah yes, now to my fortune," says Roy with an expression of curiosity and eyebrows high.

"Your fortune is at five hundred and fifty six million," says Dr. Menzel.

"Wow, and my businesses at the Travel Lodge and Don's Coffee Shops?" says Roy now beginning to wipe an old sweat off of his forehead.

"The businesses are still running. However, I'm sorry to say that a law passed forty years ago having no self profits made by business owners. The only way for owners to profit in business now is to sell the business," says Dr. Menzel looking at the computer screen showing Roy's EKG heart rhythm.

"What? I will never sell my businesses. They will be in my name until the day I die, for better or for worse," says Roy showing a serious look.

"A lot has happened in the past fifty years, people view money differently than back in the day," says Dr. Menzel.

"What do you mean?" says Roy with eyebrows down in disappointment.

"In 2035, the government passed a law changing the way people use money and conduct business. With the majority of citizens and the U.S. government being in insurmountable debt, the global economy has changed to the mind set of less is more," says Dr. Menzel.

"You mean being a multi-millionaire is not the greedy desire or dream of everyone?" says Roy.

"That is correct Roy. The American dream is having the least amount of debt and not being able to manage the most amount of debt. To look on the bright side of things, in a few hours you should be able to get out and enjoy the nice summer day," says Dr. Menzel.

"I'm hungry, I suppose I haven't eaten in fifty years. So what happened to everyone that was rich during the change in 2035?" says Roy.

"Many people had the opportunity to pay more taxes to the government to take away the burden of having so much money or debt burden. Every one is trying to get their bank accounts, stock prices, and interest rates to zero now," says Dr. Menzel.

"I need to look at today's news paper let's stop by the store and get one when we go out later," says Roy sitting upright and pulling the EKG cords off of his body.

"I will get you some casual clothes to wear," says Dr. Menzel.

"I need a matching outfit, I don't prefer wearing hospital scrubs out in public," says Roy.

Dr. Menzel hands Roy a white Ronald McDonald Charity shirt and a pair of brown jeans with holes in the knees. A look of disgust shows on Roy's face as he drapes the clothes against the front of his body.

"What is this? What kind of world is this?" says Roy.

"We're going to get some clothes at the store at our first stop," says Dr. Menzel with a look of agreement with Roy.

*   *   *

The mid day sun is high in the sky with bright rays shining through the big sky scrapers in Trenton, Minnesota. Dark shadows occur in building corners and alleys where there are few pedestrians compared to the busy sidewalks and streets. Roy wears his newly purchased casual apparel: a Coca Cola t-shirt, kaki dress pants, and sandals that are too big for his feet.

"The next time I choose a wardrobe, please let me try on the item before we buy it. Look, these sandals are hideously big," says Roy stopping his walk to point down towards his oversized sandal.

"Do you have any place you would like to go right away Roy?" says Dr. Menzel halting his walk to turn around looking at Roy.

"Yes, lets go to the public library, is it still there?" says Roy.

"Yes, it's still there, books are rarely checked out there due to everything being available in electronic format. Most of the books have been recycled," says Dr. Menzel wiping his nose with a Kleenex and tossing it into a side walk trash can.

Roy and Dr. Menzel walk the few blocks to the library from the Cryogenics Lab. The library has Greek looking pillars making up the door way and upon walking into the vast lobby; a thick dome of glass ceiling is bordered by window framing. Plants with spade shaped leaves are placed in the library hallway corridors. Only a few book shelves are present with the rest of the library having open desks. The desks have a doc station cord for personal computer use and a built in computer screen projector in the desk.

"I can't wait to see what the currency change in 2035 did to the stock market," says Roy combing his fingers through his partial head of brown hair.

"It was quite controlled actually with only a twenty-four hour transition process. The process of trading switched from rising prices of shares being a good thing to a decreasing share price being a good thing. The objective is to reach zero share price, and only the top companies in the S&P 500 are within a dollar," says Dr. Menzel sitting next to Roy at the desk.

"I don't understand, since there is a lower share price, people should be able to buy more shares of the best companies compared to the worst," says Roy with a confused look on his face.

Sitting down at the personal computer station, Roy turns on the computer monitor. His search in the archives of the Trenton Newspaper brings up front page headlines of the economic change in 2035.

"There is a certain allotment of shares able to be bought by people every year based on age. Usually, the older a person is, the more shares they can purchase. For example, I'm eighty-nine years old and this year I can purchase eighty-nine shares," says Dr. Menzel sitting down next to Roy.

By now, the computer screen switches to a colorful screensaver of the library in mid-winter. Snow is covering the stone steps with icicles hanging down the pillared roof top entrance.

"The shares are purchased with money, right? Why would someone want to pay more for a bad stock?" says Roy.

"To get rid of their debt, money is used to purchase," says Dr. Menzel.

"How does more money in stock prices affect a company?" says Roy still trying to discover how everything in the reversed economy balances out.

"Before 2035 people paid money to receive goods. Now, it's the opposite, when people get a product or service they get money put into their account too. There is no more sales tax, but there is taxes taken out of every pay check," says Dr. Menzel.

"So you are saying, since everyone viewed money as debt, the government took away the ability of the consumer to handle money in exchange for goods," says Roy realizing money is seen as a burden to have.

"Exactly, because almost everyone could not handle money responsibly. The government and most of society was in over their heads," says Dr. Menzel.

"Look, it says here that business growth dropped to five percent or less a year after 2035," says Roy looking at the screen of a newspaper article dated, March 25, 2040.

"Capitalism turned inside out. Instead of wanting money to go in, we want money to go out. How many times does it take to succeed?" says Dr. Menzel.

CHAPTER 6

"Hi, this is Sam Johnson reporting from Wall Street where an unexpected near perfect zero share price was reached today. Sting, a computer database developer was at a zero price per share for two minutes and later went to fifty cents. No company share price has ever reached zero share price since the 2035 currency shift," says Sam reporting on a radio inside a bar and grill restaurant.

Roy and Dr. Menzel sit in a booth facing each other. Roy tucks a napkin into the neck collar of his t-shirt and grabs his fork to start eating his three cheese quesadilla.

"If a company does get to zero share price, where does it go from there?" says Roy taking his first bite out of his quesadilla.

"What do you mean? Would it pass zero and be a negative number? I don't think there is that option to consider. A company will either have a share price of so many dollars or zero," says Dr. Menzel after sipping his coffee cup and dripping some coffee on the table below.

"That can't be right. Someone cannot own a thousand shares of zero dollars per share, it would not exist. Say the price increased again due to demand, it would not be feasible to have a share price value go from something to nothing," says Roy.

"I know what you are saying. If there is a zero price per share, a person can have as many free shares they want. However, remember a person is only allotted so many shares each year. It must go down to the partial penny, like .0001 cents," says Dr. Menzel using his high eyebrows and head down to emphasize the significant point he is focusing on.

"Who came up with the idea to switch our economic perception?" says Roy switching the topic of conversation.

"An economist by the name of Shelly Swenson, she was awarded the Nobel Prize. Her philosophy was picked up by every country in the world because she proved through every economic scenario that reversalism works," says Dr. Menzel wiping his mouth with his napkin and beginning to arrange each bite of food in sections, so that every bite is pre-cut and ready for him to eat.

"I'm sure some business owners did not like the idea. I look around and see healthier people with lower obesity, and people are not in a rush to do things," says Roy.

"You are right, many of the top business owners quit when the interest with creating wealth and innovating quality of life stopped. They simply stopped working and stopped trying to progress because of the equalization of work," says Dr. Menzel.

"I've got to admit the gap between the high and low income was getting pretty wide. Now, there is little growth, little progression," says Roy.

"You are right again; we have been in a recession for forty years when looking at the capitalistic view of growth. Few people without debt try out perform others now. Successful people today are people without debt not people with a lot of money. The hard workers today are people still trying to diminish their debt or abundance," says Dr. Menzel.

"This reversed capital theory should work until everyone pays there debt back. With less people working to get out of debt, inflation will drop. How is inflation affected by reversalism?" say Roy.

"Inflation is actually starting to decrease making prices go down. No body is trying to make money, they're trying to get rid of it by working, limiting the amount of goods they consume, paying taxes, and purchasing high priced stocks," says Dr. Menzel.

Walking towards their booth, a tall brown haired waitress gives a receipt of the bill coming to nine dollars and eighty nine cents.

"Can you put it on my account," says Roy handing over his driver's license from back in 2024.

"Sure, I will be right back," says the waitress with an unusual look of confusion on her face. She grabs the ID from Roy's hand, places it in the black billing wallet, and goes up to the front counter.

"I guess that nine dollars has no affect on my half a billion account value. Any ideas of how I can work my way to zero?" says Roy.

"Work as much as you can and pay Uncle Sam immensely," says Dr. Menzel.

With a smile on her face, the waitress comes back to the booth and says, "The legend standing before me. How many times does it take to succeed Roy Monte?"

CHAPTER 7

The next day, Roy sits in the Cryogenics Lab waiting lobby reading a Time Magazine article about the one hundred most influential people of the century. Roy wears a buttoned long sleeve shirt, a pair of jeans and sandals. The lobby is big enough to fit a tennis court with eight rows of cushion seats.

"You must be from around here," says a blonde hair woman in her late forties.

"Yes and no you see I was here fifty years ago and came back yesterday. My name is Roy Monte, by the way," says Roy trying to read the woman's squinty blue eye expression.

"Okay, whatever you say Roy. Talk about a culture shock, perhaps. Roy, my name is Krisa," says Krisa tucking her hair behind her left ear so she can see with her long bangs. Her black purse hangs at her side with one shoulder shrugged up to keep the purse strap from sliding off her shoulder.

"Nice to meet you Krisa," says Roy nodding to show a confirming gesture and starting to tap his sandal against the tile floor.

Two other people are seated in the lobby waiting to hear about a case of cellular freezing to treat a rare case of asthma. There is a light above each chair in the eight row lobby with an ultra thin TV on each wall tuned into the same news channel. A coffee machine and sink is located next to the exit door that leads out to the front door outside. Roy sits next to the coffee station with a cup of coffee in his hands.

"I bet you are new to the reversalism economic theory. I was five when it happened, I'll never forget the day," says Krisa.

"Please, share your story," says Roy putting down the Time Magazine and placing it on the coffee table next to his chair.

Krisa takes a seat in the row of chairs across from Roy. Pausing still, she collects her memory to begin the telling of her story. Finding the perfect memory to start, she slouches back in her chair and crosses one leg over the other.

"I was watching T.V. one evening when my father comes home from work and abruptly turns the channel to the news. President Henney was addressing the nation on the world wide agreement to adopt reversalism," says Krisa daydreaming off into the lobby wall.

"The best way to explain his reaction is he got his legs cut out from under him. He was a small business owner of a convenience store and was looking forward to another stimulus bill the government would have to pass in order to not default on the nation's debt. The stimulus helped the oil refineries get oil at cheaper price and thus sell gasoline for less money," says Krisa.

"How did it affect jobs, was there deflation?" says Roy.

"Business slowed for the first few days, but after the first couple of weeks, it resumed to normal. People received their first paycheck and things kind of went back to normal. There are those people who have those dooms day predictions and slow deflation has been occurring ever since the change," says Krisa.

"Inflation is necessary for economic growth, when will government officials realize this is the right decision to make?" says Roy.

"Every person is for them self, this is the case in a free enterprise system. The ability to handle money no longer exists. It is taken take care of for us now. If I want something, say a new car. I will need to choose wisely between my given allotments," says Krisa.

"What happened to your Father and his convenience store? Did he continue to operate it?" says Roy.

Now, the only two people in the lobby are Krisa and Roy. With the TV and humming of the ventilation entering through a ceiling vent creating a distraction, Roy focuses on the picture of a lion jumping at the person viewing it, as if it were to come alive and jump out at Roy.

After searching for what to say, Krisa says, "My father ran that convenience store into the ground. The last drop of gas was pumped out of that station eight months after the reversal."

"I'm sorry to hear about that Krisa," says Roy while placing his hand over his mouth while looking into Krisa's eyes as she recalls the days leading up to her fathers store closure.

"You have no idea how hard he worked to get that, years it was. We must let them know, how many times will it take to get this point across to government officials and succeed?" says Krisa.

CHAPTER 8

"Come on baby! I need a miracle," says a middle aged man sitting at the casino's slot machine. He has long brown hair and facial hair.

"Look at this place its packed," says Roy walking through the enormous Trenton Casino with slot machines and card tables on the lower level and a dance area on the second floor where a live celebrity performance is occurring.

"After the 2035 Reversal, casino's sprung up everywhere in the U.S. Instead of trying to win money, they are a ticket to quickly get rid of wealth. Even the billionaire Bill Rivet won a billion dollar dream withdrawal from his account," says Krisa wearing a pair of blue jeans and white button up shirt.

"Tell me, how does this gambling to get rid of debt work?" says Roy wearing an orange stripe t-shirt and tan kaki's. Black sun glasses make his face less noticeable with them fitting to his eyes perfectly.

"A person chooses how many gambling chips they want at the front desk, the more chips they get, the more money gets put onto their account," says Krisa.

"So just like a person paying money to gamble, now a person gets money put onto their account to gamble. Being a winner at a gambling game, the person can bring the chips to the front desk and have that amount taken out their account," says Roy with a voice of enthusiasm.

"Exactly, to take money out of the account, they must work, join the military, win the lottery, or win in a gamble," says Krisa.

"In my businesses, the ones I owned in 2024, I looked for having expenses to be equal or less than my income," says Roy being interrupted by Krisa.

"Businesses look to have more expenses than income. A business owner will have money put into the business account each month until they've paid all the money the building or land is worth. This way, there is no default on payments," says Krisa.

The bartender on the lower level stands in front of a man and woman mixing drinks and looks up to wink one eye at Krisa. Making it look easy, the bartender with one bottle in each hand, spins them each on his index fingers. He grabs the spinning bottles simultaneously and pours them both in a drinking glass.

"Well, are you feeling lucky?" says Krisa with a wide smile putting her hand on Roy's shoulder.

"Funny, back in the day money would just slip through my fingers. Now, it sticks to my fingers like super glue. I will do twenty dollars of slots that's it," says Roy.

Walking out of the Trenton Casino, Roy and Krisa enter the cool night air. The casino's circle drive has a water fountain shooting up out of the pool twenty feet into the air. Lights at the bottom of the pool of water make the ripples of water shine brightly.

"Well, I'm sure better off with the three hundred dollars that's been deducted from my account," says Krisa walking in front of Roy and looking behind while walking forward.

"I suppose since you were a child when the reversal hit your account is near zero," says Roy placing his hands in the side pockets of his kakis and casually walking.

"Not quite, I just had Lasik eye surgery costing more than a few thousand," says Krisa.

Krisa stops at a bench on the lawn next to the water fountain and Roy sits next to her. The bench faces the casino with the fountain behind them. The big lights light up every window of the three floor casino building. A red sign in front of the casino says: "Trenton Treasure Land", with flashing yellow lights around the words.

"I had a good time tonight Krisa," says Roy.

"It's great to show you around, let me know when you want to get out again," says Krisa with a wide smile.

A taxi pulls up and Roy walks around the car to the back passenger seat. Driving away, Krisa is left looking at the red and yellow lights of the sign flashing before her eyes.

*   *   *

"Hello, this is Get Rid of Your Wealth for Better Health Services," says the receptionist.

"Yes, my name is Roy and would like to get some advice by phone," says Roy on the phone and sitting in the lobby at the hospital.

"Sure, my name is Erica, what advice do you seek?" says Erica.

"I never thought I would be saying this, how do I get rid of my accounts wealth?" says Roy having a pen and piece of paper on his lap ready to write.

"Well, work hard and live within your means, did you know? The government will take more money out of your account each year if you can score a thirty credit score by living within your means," says Erica.

"Okay, I'll take note of that," say Roy writing down 'hard work and living below means' on his piece of paper.

Rolling his eyes, Roy says, "Thanks for your advice, I'll be sure to keep that in mind. How about gambling?"

"Very few people get that lucky Roy," says Erica.

"Hey, I hear you, but a little can go a long way. Have a good day Erica," says Roy ending the conversation.

"Bye Roy, I hope to meet you in person," says Erica hanging up the line on a cordless phone attached to the wall. Showing a little effort, Roy goes back to sit down in the lobby chair by letting his lower body buckle at the knees and hips to basically fall into the chair.

*   *   *

"One for the money, two for the show, come on wealth let's go, go, go!" says Roy at the Trenton Casino slot machine.

Getting nothing from the spin, Roy looks down at his feet resting on the bar stool chair. He taps his foot rhythmically on the foot rest and his right hand grips the slot machine handle so tight a rubbing noise occurs. His palms are sweaty and the veins begin to pop out in his hands and forearms.

"Why me? I had good intentions and worked so hard to get my wealth. Now, the best thing I had going for myself is against me," says Roy to himself with eyes squinting and looking down.

"Hey man did you win?" says a stranger with an Irish accent, black sun glasses, and a Hawaiian shirt.

The stranger has the same lanky body type and height of Roy. His hair comes down to his side burns.

"Do you want some help? Don't ya know I have the luck of the Irish with me. I won just the other day ya know. Me name is Walton Dinnly," says Walton putting his hand in front of him to shake hands.

"Would you like some help? What they don't tell ya is that focusing on one slot increases the chances of winning. At least that is how I win," says Walton.

A black haired woman having a purple shirt, shorts, and sandals approaches Roy and Walton, grabbing Walton's hand. As she swings her hand by her side, she looks up at Walton. They clearly know each other intimately with their flirting smile as they look at each other.

"Well, who's your friend?" says the woman.

"This is my wife Becky, what ever she says, don't believe it," says Walton with an expression of sarcasm.

"Like the time you were at the Daytona Beach and did what the para sailing instructor told you to do. Use your body to lean against the sail. Yeah, then you did a face plant into water by leaning into the sail, instead of against it," says Becky chuckling under her breath and holding her hand over her mouth.

"Now when he told me 'against' I thought he meant push into it," says Walton.

Roy laughs and says, "That's hilarious, here's one for you. There was a Norwegian and Palestinian getting married. Later, when they had their first child they named it Yahsir Youbetcha."

Walton and Becky laugh and walk towards the front row slot machines. Roy is left with his last slot spin, so he spins it and it comes up with nothing. Roy walks over to the bar to sit in front of the same bartender who winked at Krisa the night before.

"Hey, it's you again? What can I put together for you today?" says the bartender.

"Tap water please, what's your name? My name is Roy," says Roy wiping his lips with his right forearm.

"My name is Barney, but everyone calls me Bub," says Barney.

Barney wears a white dress shirt and red bow tie with thick black curly hair extending down to his eye brows.

"How long have you been here working at the casino Barney?" says Roy.

"I've been here for ten years and been succeeding for the last two years. Eight years it took me to succeed, how many times does it take to succeed?" says Barney.

"Depends on the variables, and no matter the variables, anything that happens seems to never be enough," says Roy taking a drink of his glass of water.

CHAPTER 9

"Krisa, are we there yet?" says Roy riding in Krisa's black Mercedes sports car.

"Almost, just a few more blocks. I can't wait to show you my African violet, it's so big. My collection of Shaun Sikes paintings is quite vast," says Amanda driving through an intersection with cars honking from behind as she changes lanes abruptly.

"Wow, this is unsafe driving. Please, don't do that again," says Roy with both hands covering his eyes from the traffic.

"That one came up by surprise, I'll check my blind spot next time," says Krisa with a wide smile on her face and tucking her blonde hair behind her ear.

"Who in the world is Shaun Sikes?" says Roy.

"He's a famous artist who did the famous "Yo-Yo" painting, you should have seen it. The painting literally makes your eyes think the person was moving and unwinding a yo-yo on a string. He created the effect by drawing a series of faded yo-yo's, it was so cool," says Krisa driving into her driveway.

At Krisa's house, the "s" shaped driveway circles around her two story home, leading to the garage in the back yard.

Krisa and Roy exit the car parked in the garage and walk up the porch deck into the homes interior.

The house has many windows, lights, and two Victorian chandeliers in the dining and living room area. Lights hang on the wall from a chain every five feet, and a big shudder window on the east and south wall.

"Wow, what happened? How did you acquire this nice of home with the reversal economy?" says Roy.

"Have a seat at the dining table and I'll tell you Roy," says Krisa sitting down at the round dining table with eight chairs.

The marble tile floors light purple color has a dim reflection from the lights. Krisa leans forward, placing her forearms and fingers interlocked on the clear glass dining table. If it wasn't for the small table cloth and Victorian candle holders, her full reflection from the glass could be fully seen on the table's surface by Roy sitting across from her.

"Roy, I have looked up to you for many years upon hearing about you in a history class. From that point on, I decided to emulate you. It's quite possible to have abundance in the reversal economic system I simply did what you did, work," says Krisa raising both palms in the air to make it obvious the point she was making.

"I have all this money and the logical way to get rid of it is work. I've done that enough in my life; I don't want to go through it again. I worked to get the money, why should I have to work in order to get rid of it?" says Roy.

"All this money will be a burden acting as a monkey on your back. You're up for a come back Roy. What do you say?" says Krisa.

"I say a person can either work to live or live to work. Or can a person live to work and live at the same time?" says Roy.

"If a person likes the work they do, they will never have to work a day in their life," says Krisa interweaving her fingers through her hair.

Pausing, Roy looks above Krisa's head at a digital clock on the wall. The second the clock changes from six o nine to six ten time stops. Right then and there, Roy makes his decision on what to do next.

"Let's go to work," says Roy with a serious game face.

"Let's get the resume out there," says Krisa pointing to the front door.

Looking out the window next to the front door, Roy looks at the lawn, which has been mowed in two different directions.

"We should go outside for a walk Krisa," says Roy standing up.

"I will show you my rock garden," says Krisa.

The day is nice and sunny with a slight breeze to make the trees sway a little side to side. Roy and Krisa, walk on the sod lawn having a criss-cross look in two directions. The rock garden is located about a hundred yards from the house with a stone sidewalk leading to it. On each side of the side walk there are hedge bushes cut flat at the top extending up to the height of Krisa and Roy's shoulders.

"This is beautiful, how many acres do you have back here?" says Roy looking around at the vast back yard lawn with the rock garden at the outskirts of a dense woods of oak trees.

"There is ten acres total, most of it is a wooded area that you see on the other side of the rock wall," says Krisa pointing to the wooded area she is referring to while walking next to Roy.

"Looking back on my life, I've often wondered what has been most meaningful. I have lived to work my entire adult life and now I'm getting to the end of my working years," says Roy.

"Are you looking for something else to do besides work?" says Krisa trying to reiterate what Roy is saying while looking up with her blue eyes. By looking up, she gives a fake role play of lying.

"There is always something to do; I'm just trying to figure out what is the most meaningful task to do right now. I want to start another business, but how do I help the most people by doing it?" says Roy.

"I would say starting a non for profit business where most of the income goes back into the business for growth," says Krisa.

By now, they both are at the front hedge entrance of the rock garden. A tall alter arch surrounds the entrance of the garden. Being full of small rock beds, there is lime stone rocks, marble, Safire, gem stone, granite, big boulder rock, creosote, and iron ore. The rock garden has a twenty yard radius with the stone sidewalk mazing throughout. The biggest rock is the boulder rock standing twelve feet tall and six foot radius.

"Wow look at that wonderful looking rock," says Roy pointing over the marble rock bed.

The bed is stocked with golf ball sized marble rock having an eye looking reflection in each individual rock.

"Yes, this is one of my favorite displays due to the fact the bed seeming to move as you change your position of angle to it," says Krisa.

"I see your point of a non for profit business being a fair selection for a venture, but I'm a venture capitalist. Even if capitalism does not exist, I will seek profit. There is no thrill and excitement to work hard if you can't receive a big and worthy reward. I want to be rewarded for what I do," says Roy.

"Sometimes, the only person to decide whether or not you are great is you Roy. The critiques often do not see you behind the scenes putting in the long hours of overtime to get the job done," says Krisa facing Roy and looking him square in the eyes.

"I couldn't agree with you more. I shall be going now," says Roy turning away to walk back to the house, with Krisa walking slowly behind.

"Speaking of reward, profit is not the only reward a person can have you know? Look for rewards other than money," says Krisa.

*   *   *

The next day, Roy walks the sidewalk on Main Avenue in Trenton. His leather back pack and trench coat help to block the cool fall wind. Roy walks into One Pro Bank to the teller's desk. The tapping of his black leather shoes makes him noticeable from everyone else as their shoes do not make any noise while walking.

"Hi, my name is Roy, I'm looking to see if you're hiring and would like to give you my resume," says Roy handing his resume to the tall brown haired teller.

"Roy, you can submit an application online as we do have some positions available," says the teller.

"Great, I mean sounds great. Uh, thanks for your time," says Roy before turning around to leave the bank through revolving doors.

Next, Roy goes to a convenience store where gasoline is two eighty-seven a gallon. The store is a twenty foot by twenty foot room with an entrance and exit door on each side of the desk.

"What can I do for you?" says the woman standing at the cash register with a nose ring and braided hair.

"Yeah, I'm pursuing self actualization, I've done it before and I know I can do it again," says Roy with a serious face.

"Actualization, sounds rare alright, to me self actualization is where a person fully develops their full potential and capabilities," says the cashier behind the desk.

"Exactly, that's exactly what it is, along with going on to create works of gigantic proportions," says Roy.

While looking at the power ball board showing thirty-seven million dollars, Roy day dreams with the thought of winning it to get his account to zero.

"I'm looking to see if you are hiring, if so, what positions are available?" says Roy.

"Yeah, here is an application. I'm not sure if the position is over nights or evenings, but I know one is available. If you're in the pursuit of self actualization, I don't see how you will get it by working here." says the cashier reaching down to pull open a drawer containing the applications.

"Do not tell me that I can't do something. I will have to take matters into my own hands in the pursuit of self actualization. Doing it with the hands that god gave me," says Roy shaking both hands by his ears with palms facing forward.

"Okay, okay, whatever rocks your boat," says the cashier acting in defense of not offending Roy.

"Thanks," says Roy grabbing the application and placing it in his back pack. Putting his back pack on his back, Roy exits the store. The door bell rings as he opens the door to leave.

*   *   *

Walking into a pet store, Roy walks around a big inflatable dog at the entrance with the checkout at the store's east wall. A thin male in his late teens is at the register with wireless head phones blaring at full volume.

"Hello, my name is Roy, I'm inquiring about the sign on the door about hiring part time," says Roy.

At first, the cashier frowns his eyebrows and smiles at the same time with the music being too loud, not being able to hear Roy. Upon taking one ear piece out of one ear, he raises his eyebrows and continues to smile. The store is completely empty with no customers.

"Sorry, what was that?" says the cashier.

"I'm inquiring about the opening position for hiring. What hours are the positions?" says Roy.

"Yeah, the position is weekends during the day time, here is an application. My name is Adam, I'm the managers son," says Adam wearing a red bib over his white collared shirt, the bib has a waist pouch full of pens and a writing pad.

Roy takes the application and pauses for a brief moment while looking over its contents. There is no one in the store, so there is no one going to be buying items any time soon. Looking up at the cashier with a smile, Roy recognizes Adam is at full attention with his music turned off.

"Question, how many jobs do you work at?" says Roy.

"Just this job, I'm a full time college student," says Adam.

"Ah, I've been there. Is there still too many career options to choose from?" says Roy.

"Yeah," says Adam.

"When you work here, would you say you work so that you can live the life you want or live so you can work as if it were the most important aspect to you?" says Roy.

"I definitely work to live the life I want," says Adam.

"You work to live today's lifestyle, not the other way around. Or have you ever thought about working and living today for a better tomorrow?" says Roy.

"The tomorrow I'm striving for is not likely to occur with what I'm doing right now. Therefore, unless I do some other type of work, a better tomorrow will not happen. I want to have the best future possible, but the aspect of working for big money does not exist for someone in college," says Adam.

"Do you have a piece of paper?" says Roy pulling a pen out of his pocket.

"Here you go," says Adam handing Roy a blank piece of writing pad paper from his bib pouch.

Drawing a house with a front door and two windows on each side, Roy holds the piece of paper at shoulder height so Adam can see it.

"What is this picture of?" says Roy.

"It's a house," says Adam.

"Whose house is it?" says Roy.

Adam frowns confusingly with a pause. Roy points towards his chest with his index finger.

"Mine, it's my house I created it, right?" says Roy.

"Exactly," says Adam understanding the point Roy is making.

"Here you go, on the back side of this piece of paper, you draw a picture of your dream of a better tomorrow. Whose is it? When did you create it," says Roy with enthusiasm.

"It's my dream, and I created it today," says Adam.

"If you created it today, then you can start working to get it today. A person can go to work today and every day after that to achieve a better tomorrow, to achieve their dream," says Roy.

Leaving the store with the application in hand, Roy nods slightly downward to show a nonverbal good bye to Adam.

After Roy leaves Adam says to himself, "What an optimist."

* * *

Sitting in a coffee shop similar to Don's Coffee shop, Roy reads the *Wall Street Journal* with a cup of coffee in front of him. Suddenly his cell phone rings and he takes his palm size phone out of his pocket and answers it.

"Hi, this is Roy," says Roy answering the cell phone.

"Roy, my name is Todd Jameson. I'm returning a phone call I received yesterday evening," says Todd in a deep monotone voice.

"Oh, I was looking into your ad on the net about being able to fake death. Your Habix pills supposedly stop your heart rate for seventy two hours to be reported as dead," says Roy.

"Yes, it's the faking of the death that's the hard part. I suggest including a death note inside your pocket when doing it," says Todd.

"Great, when can I order them?" says Roy.

"We have to do this in person, do you know where the Tim's Timber is on the East side of town?" says Todd.

"Yes, I've been there before," says Roy.

"I will meet you there at midnight to go through the details," says Todd.

"See you then, I'll be sure to set my alarm clock to get some shut eye in the mean time. No, wait I set two alarm clocks," says Roy.

"In that case, you might as well set three alarm clocks, set the alarm clock for the alarm clock for the alarm clock," says Todd laughing and then hanging up the phone.

*   *   *

Five minutes before midnight, Roy pulls into the front parking lot being given a ride by taxi cab. There is one patio light in front of the Tim's Timber Lumber Yard with three yard lights located in the back.

"Would you like me to leave and come back in about a half hour?" says the cab driver.

"Yes, that would work perfectly, thanks," says Roy getting out of the cab.

The cab turns around in a u-turn out of the lumber yard parking lot. All is quiet with owls hooting in the night. A man in an Ohio State Letter jacket appears from the far side of the building.

"Roy, my name is Todd Jameson. I have your requested pills, there's eight of them in this bottle," says Todd with side burns and mustache, holding up a bottle of pills.

Roy walks over to Todd with money coins in his pocket making a jingle with each step he takes. Grinding gravel occurs after each jingle as each step digs into the loose ground. Todd holds out his hand, Roy grabs the top cover of the pill bottle, and Todd smiles to make his silver crowned teeth show with a toothpick tucked in his cheek.

"It's five hundred dollars worth onto your account. I just need your account number so I can put the money onto it," says Todd.

"Here's the account number," says Roy handing Todd a piece of paper and grabbing the bottle of pills simultaneously to complete the exchange.

"Thanks Roy, perhaps we'll meet again," says Todd turning around with a smile on his face.

With Todd vanishing behind the far side of the building, Roy takes a few of the pills and waits for them to take effect. He guzzles a bottle of purified water in fifteen seconds.

"Come on, innovation creates your future. How many times does it take to succeed?" says Roy to himself while looking up at the cloudy night sky.

Becoming dizzy and light headed, Roy kneels on one knee and falls face first onto the dirty pavement. Dust picks up around Roy when he lands. His head is rotated so his left cheek is resting on the pavement, which allows him to see the taxi lights coming from down the street to pick him up.

CHAPTER 10

"I hope you come up with a way to resolve your reputation. After that stunt you pulled, not many people are going to want to hire you," says Krisa sitting in the restaurant booth with a tall glass of ice tea in front of her.

"I thought if I was pronounced dead my account would not exist. If I can cryogenically freeze myself, why not fake my death?" says Roy eating a taco and bean side dish.

"How would you have made it long enough to be buried alive? The doctor said you woke up within minutes of arriving in the emergency center. You had nothing wrong with you and your blood had a drug called Lennux. Where did you get the drug?" says Krisa with concern.

"The Lennux pill I took turned out to be not strong enough; I should have taken eight hundred more milligrams. I got it from a private dealer on a back door deal," says Roy looking down in embarrassment.

"Work, why can't you just work like you did over fifty years ago?" says Krisa with a look of desperation.

"I can't take that anymore, both psychologically and physically I have aced that way to greatness and now, I want to find a different way. Besides, I'm old now with not much time," says Roy.

"Trying to erase your existence is almost impossible to do with the DNA and eye scans," says Krisa.

"Krisa, that is why I'm going to do it," says Roy.

Eating the final bite of his taco, Roy grabs his fork to start consuming the beans. He looks at Krisa with a surprising look as if something miraculous is about to happen.

"I have come up with a way to change my identity, I will wear a special contact lens to deter the eye scanners and take special pills to change my blood DNA," says Roy.

"What will be your new name?" says Krisa.

"My new name will be Ken Carson," says Roy.

The restaurant waitress approaches the table to check on their value of the food. She wears a black dress shirt and pants, red hair, and a food tray at her left shoulder. Her deep blue eyes and wide nose catch a person's attention right away.

"How is everything today?" says the waitress.

"Great, we were just saying how this delicious food has made our day," says Roy.

The waitress smiles and leaves the dining area. Krisa and Roy pause to try remember where they left off in their conversation.

"Ken, sounds like a Barbie name," says Krisa.

"Shut it!" says Roy in sarcasm with a smile on his face.

"I was just trying to help out," says Krisa.

Looking up at the clock, it is ten pm. Krisa moves sideways while seated out of the booth to a standing position. Roy stands next and the two pay for their meals and walk out of the restaurant into the dimly lit street.

*   *   *

"I can't wait that long Sam, I need this ID card and account set up by tomorrow," says Roy sitting in the front seat of a public transportation bus talking on his phone.

"I will do my best; it's the ID card that I'm most worried about. A creator is required and that person is usually a federal employee. If authorities look into your file they might see a fake creator name and become suspicious," says Sam on the other line.

"Well Sam, with the amount I'm hiring you for, it better be done within the next forty-eight hours. Will Ken's account have a history?" says Roy.

"You will be from Italy relocating to U.S. eight years ago and recently obtaining citizenship here in the country. I will look and see about finding a federal employee for the creator name," says Sam.

"Anything I should know about the account?" says Roy.

"The account is the easy part, I have connections with a brokerage firm that creates accounts for bankrupt clients. I basically forged Ken's signature for a bankruptcy on his ID card on new citizenship," says Sam.

Pausing the conversation with the bus coming to a stop, Roy looks up at the bus driver's face in the rear view mirror. The bus driver looks at Roy and smiles.

"I'm worried that some people may already know me by name Sam. How do I deter people from recognizing me as Roy? Every time I go some place my ID is scanned showing my name," says Roy to Sam on the phone.

"I suggest you shave your head, grow out your facial hair, and wear sunglasses to change your appearance.

If there have been places gone to regularly since the unfreezing, stop going there," says Sam.

"I'll take that into consideration, the pick up will occur tomorrow evening then. How about some where outside the city?" says Roy.

"Yeah, there is gas station on highway fifty-six going west. I will be there waiting at twenty-three hundred hours," says Sam.

"Okay, see you then," says Roy.

Roy hangs up his phone and places his index finger to his left temple having thoughts about tomorrow night. The bus is full with only three seats in the front open. Sitting in the outside seat in the fourth row, Roy pulls the stopping line above him to signal for the next stop.

*   *   *

Going into the BP gas station at ten-forty five in the evening, Roy is dressed in a tight fitted t-shirt and loosely fitted sweat pants. His skinny frame makes his upper body look disproportion compared to his lower body. Getting some black licorice, Roy leaves the station exit door while passing a female police officer.

"Excuse me sir, have you seen this fellow?" says the police officer with black hair in a pony tail.

Roy keeps the exit door held open with his arm and looks at the wanted photo and name Sam Gosen printed on the bottom.

"Nope, doesn't look familiar," says Roy shaking his head looking at the photo.

"He's wanted for fraud and was last seen yesterday three miles away on the outskirts of Trenton," says the officer with a look of suspicion towards Roy.

"I hope you get him," says Roy walking past the officer towards Dr. Menzel's black car.

At approximately eleven pm a red pick up truck pulls into the gas station from the high way. The truck drives right by the parked police car as the female police officer is exiting the station doors.

Sam in the truck pulls up to park along side Roy waiting in the black car. Once the cop leaves the station, Sam and Roy both leave their vehicles to meet in front of the red truck. Sam is a big muscular man with a bald head and thin mustache. His tight black shirt and baggy red shorts look like he is ready for a gym workout.

"Roy, I have the ID in this envelope along with the contacts and DNA changing pills," says Sam handing over a golden eight by eleven inch envelope to Roy.

"How many pills do I take?" says Roy.

"All three need to be taken in this order and one hour apart. First, take the green pill; an hour later, take the yellow pill; another hour later, take the red pill to complete the change to your DNA. The change is irreversible so don't plan on becoming Roy Monte again," says Sam whispering to Roy.

"Thanks, and do you know the police are after you?" says Roy.

"What is new? They've been after me for years, how many times will it take for them to succeed in catching me?" says Sam expressing as if it will never happen.

Sam gets into the pickup truck and drives away as Roy opens the envelope to look over the contents inside the folder. The pills at the bottom of the big envelope are all the same shape and size with one green, red, and yellow pill.

CHAPTER 11

"Okay, that should do the trick," says Roy taking the red pill while looking at his wrist watch to time an hour exactly.

Sitting in the car with the driver's door open, Ken's (Roy Monte) cell phone rings, he stands up to take his cell phone out of his front pant pocket.

"Hi, this is Ken," says Ken answering the phone.

"Ken, I have a proposition for you. There is an open office space just down the street from my house, do you want to look at it?" says Dr. Menzel pulling his long blonde hair away from his face.

"Hmmm, I've identified a need to fill and am eager to brainstorm some possibilities." says Ken.

"With your entrepreneurial spirit, anything can happen," says Dr, Menzel opening his big lower jaw to yawn.

"What I'll do is meet you at my Travel Lodge Hotel in the morning for a continental breakfast. How does seven thirty sound?" says Ken.

"Great Roy, I mean Ken," says Dr. Menzel.

*   *   *

"I bet you weren't expecting me this early, were you?" says Dr, Menzel sitting in the breakfast diner around seven in the morning.

Dr. Menzel is wearing a green collared golf shirt. His hair is combed to the right side and a cup of coffee sits in front of him. A notebook and pen is to the right of his coffee.

"Please wait, I'm starving for one of the new chefs fresh waffles, I'll be right back," says Ken going up to the self serve line to get a plate of waffles.

Sitting across the table from Dr. Menzel, Ken puts syrup on his waffles shaking powdered sugar on top.

"So how big is this space your talking of on the phone doctor," says Roy taking his first bite of waffle.

"A thousand square feet," says Dr. Menzel.

"Huh, here is my idea, it relates to me. I see many people including me trying to get their accounts to zero. To solve this, I will start a credit card company that pulls two dollars out of an individuals account for every one dollar that's in it," says Ken.

Pausing, Dr. Menzel thinks about the business idea with deep thought.

"How will this work? As a business you will go bankrupt. How will you break even?" says Dr. Menzel taking a drink of coffee.

"I will charge a small start up fee and use selling shares and time as my ally. It will be first come first serve for one thousand people a year. There will be borrowing money into the company and getting money back out to clients at the end of the month," says Ken cutting a big chunk of waffle with his fork and taking a big bite.

Dr. Menzel shows a face of misunderstanding and astonishing disbelief. Again, he yawns and drinks his coffee. After sipping his coffee he shakes his head and smiles.

"The numbers add up over time, you see I will create my own exchange of shares in the stock market with three different entities. They are selling, buying, and holding. What causes the share prices to rise and fall in the stock market?" says Ken.

"When people sell shares more often than buy, the share price falls and vice versa," says Dr. Menzel.

"Exactly, and just as I have made my money buying rising shares, I can get people to lose their money with falling shares. The business mission will be to get rid of peoples money in the stock market and sell the falling shares at the end of the year for the business to break even," says Ken.

"This place will act as a brokerage firm with intentions to time the market to get rid of money or to gain money," says Dr. Menzel.

"Yep and I will be more likely to succeed with more customers. For example, the first year I charge a hundred dollar start up fee and pull two thousand dollars from an account while putting one thousand dollars back into it at monthly increments. If I get ten thousand customers in a year, there will be a quarter of a million dollars I can get rid of," says Ken writing an income and expense column on Dr. Menzel's note book paper.

"Paying one thousand dollars to each of the thousand customers at years end will get rid of a million dollars. Will the securities and exchange commission allow such rapid buying and selling?" says Dr. Menzel.

"They will embrace this with arms wide open," says Ken finishing his last bite of the waffle and drinking the rest of his orange juice.

*   *   *

"Hi, is this the Trenton University?" says Ken on the phone standing in the empty office space down the street from Dr. Menzel's house.

"Yes it is, how can I help you?" says the college office administrator.

"I would like to put up a job opening for your soon to be graduated finance students this year, as I'm looking for highly qualified employees," says Ken.

"I certainly will tell the finance faculty of your need. Will you best be reached at this number?" says the administrator.

"Yes, this number is perfect during weekday business hours, thanks, good bye," says Ken hanging up the phone and putting it in his pocket.

"Tell the landlord we will take the space for rent Doctor," says Ken to Dr. Menzel.

The one thousand foot office space is empty with three metal pillars spaced evenly in the middle to divide the room. Unfinished electrical and telephone wires hang down from the ceiling to the tile floor.

"Well, we need desks, chairs, computers, and phones," says Dr. Menzel standing on the other side of the room to Ken.

"Let's go shopping, I wonder how many times it will take for this business to succeed?" says Ken walking to the front door of the empty office.

"It's going to take every day that it is open for business. With an all or nothing effort there is no truer way to achieve success," says Dr. Menzel looking out of the office window next to the front entrance door.

Black birds scatter about the pavement of the outside parking lot looking for worms and bugs after the recent rainfall earlier in the day.

CHAPTER 12

"If you don't mind me asking, where are you getting the financing for this new business venture Ken?" says Dr. Menzel.

"With my new account and identity, I was able to start out with a good reputation for money at the bank," says Ken walking with the Doctor into an office retail store.

"Okay, I say we will need a dozen of each item. Maybe they will have same day delivery on that big of an order," says Dr. Menzel.

Walking up to a store employee with long curly hair and Pearl printed on her name tag, Ken shows his list of four items of twelve each.

"Looks like you have a room to fill," says Pearl squinting her blue eyes so she can read the hand writing.

"Attention shoppers the store will be closing in ten minutes. Please proceed to the checkout as soon as possible," says a voice over the stores intercom.

"I can place the order today, and get it out the door tomorrow. Please write the address here," says Pearl handing over the order form attached to a clipboard.

*   *   *

A week later, the furniture is in and the studio is finalized and ready to go. The logo signage next to the entrance door says, "Exuberant Ways".

"Okay, let's get started," says Roy to his four new employees huddled in a circle in the office.

"I like what you've done with the place," says a gentleman with a British accent wearing a business suit and tie standing at the front door.

Ken looks back over his shoulder towards the front door. The gentleman has Irish red hair and thick side burns. His body is darkened with shadow from the light beaming into the front windows. The ceiling lights are turned off because of the significant amount of outside light coming through the windows.

"Hi, what can we do for you sir? My name is Ken Carson," says Ken.

"Ken, my name is Timothy Kash, I seen your ad online and would like to be one of your clients," says Timothy with duffle bag hanging on his shoulder.

"Ah, just in time while we are just getting started. Here, step into my office and have a seat Tim," says Ken gesturing his hand towards his office door.

Opening the wooden door to his office, Roy and Timothy walk into the eight by ten foot room with shades pulled down. The door closes behind Roy, shaking the door glass.

"Ken I have fifty grand to get rid of, what can you do for me?" says Timothy while sweeping the left index finger under his nose.

Taking out a diagram, Ken reads explanations of each category, "Well we have the monthly payment plan, which takes a chunk of money out of your account each month. The variable plan works best for those who are on the verge of bankruptcy or foreclosure at the government set one million dollar mark."

"Well, I don't think I need that as I'm not close to that," says Timothy.

"No worries, you're in a better situation than a person I know well. You're situation is very doable," says Ken.

"I have no idea what would work best in my case," says Timothy.

"We start off taking say five hundred dollars out of your account per month and invest it in some companies whose share prices are going down in value. At the end of one year, we will sell half the shares loosing value and reinvest the remainder to lose more value the following year," says Ken writing one thousand dollars and an arrow pointing to five hundred dollars one year later.

A balancing sun dial sits on Ken's desk next to his name tag. The air duct above creates a humming noise from the air vent overhead. Ken circles the five hundred dollar word twice to emphasize to Timothy the difference it will make using this approach.

"Sounds good, let's give it a shot. Here is my account number," says Timothy with sincere confidence in his eyes.

*   *   *

"Juan, does the new financial program have more options for converting a single account into a family account?" says a female coworker working across the cubicle desk from Juan.

"You will have to pull up there account and under the payment tab check the convert member account. Do you see what I'm saying Matilda?" says Juan.

Juan has a goatee and deep sunken in eyes. He looks like he has been up all night doing work. Matilda wears a purple shirt and black jeans; the purple clothing matches her purple hair highlights.

"Sandy, where are you going at this hour?" says Juan talking to Sandy in her mid twenties, blond hair, and five and a half feet tall. She moves in quick stride about to walk out of the front office door.

"I forgot something in my car, I'll be right back," says Sandy halting her walk to the door and turning to square her body to everyone. She smiles to make her eyebrows and lips widen before turning around to push the front door open.

"Okay gang, our goal for this month is sixty clients that's two clients a day. I will be on call every day when we're not in business. Juan, where are we currently at?" says Ken talking to everyone in front of the four cubicles in the studio.

"Two," says Juan rotating his wrist watch one hundred eighty degrees.

"Great, we've met our quota for the day, but don't stop there. Be all you can be," says Ken wearing a black business suit, red tie, black sunglasses, a grown beard, and a shaved head.

"Oh, and one question," says a women raising her hand.

"Yes April," says Ken pointing in her direction.

"Are there any ways I can increase my income or wages with work performance here?" says April.

April wears eye glasses loosely on her face so they rest at the tip of her nose. A hair clip keeps her brown hair up on top of her head. Interlocking her fingers together at her front knee with crossed legs, makes her look focused on what Ken is saying. She bounces her bottom heel off the ground in a quick rhythm.

"Yes, there is a ten percent commission for each client's original investment. This commission will be deducted from your account with your paycheck," says Ken.

"My online marketing should draw some people in, Juan is putting together some bill boards, and Matilda is working on an upcoming T.V. commercial," says April pushing her glasses up closer to her face.

"Yes, the commercial headline is: 'Be a hero, let's get your account to zero'," says Matilda.

"How about you Juan?" says Ken.

"My billboard is going to show a picture of a man doing a hand stand with a message at the bottom saying, 'Got Zero?'" says Juan.

"Fancy Juan, that shall do great. Now, I know we are just starting and things are going to be a little slow at times but hang in there. Hang in there until that clock over there turns to the top of the final hour. Did you know that Colonel Sanders filed for bankruptcy at least a half dozen times before succeeding?" says Ken.

"Who is Colonel Sanders?" says Sandy walking through the door in time to listen the last part of Ken's speech.

"Colonel Sanders is the entrepreneur who started the Kentucky Fried Chicken franchise. Do any of you know who Colonel Sanders is?" says Ken looking around to see that no one has any reconciliation of Colonel Sanders.

"I know who Donald Trump is," says Sam.

Deprivational Mean

That is another good example. This is a great start but every day is a challenge and we need to ask ourselves periodically. How many times does it take to succeed?" says Ken hanging up his black business suit, rolling up the white arm sleeves, and loosening his neck tie. He walks into his office and closes the door.

CHAPTER 13

"Exuberant Ways this is Matilda," says Matilda answering the phone.

"Yes, I'm calling on behalf of the United States Federal Bureau of Investigation and looking to see if Ken Carson is available," says the woman on the other line.

"Oh yes, he's in his office, would you like me to transfer you?" says Matilda with eyebrows raised in surprise while turning her eyes to look towards Ken's office.

"That's okay I'll talk to him in a bit, bye," says the FBI women hanging up the phone.

Within a split second of hanging up the phone two Federal Agents walk into the studio. Both men wearing ear pieces, white dress shirt, red tie, and black sun glasses. One is smaller with bald head looking to be in his late thirties, the other walking last through the door is big and tall with long black hair pulled back into a pony tail.

Ken sees the men through his office window and stands up out of his chair before the Federal Agents get to his office door.

Without knocking, the Agents enter Ken's office. They're twice the size of Ken and ready to act on their intentions. Immediately, they shut the door behind them.

"Ken Carson, I'm detective Rodriguez and this is detective Schmidt," says the smaller bald agent Rodriguez.

"We are here today regarding the missing identity of Roy Monte. He was cryogenically unfrozen a couple of months ago and hasn't been seen in a few weeks," says agent Schmidt.

Ken sits back down in his leather office chair and puts his feet up on the desk.

"Haven't heard of the guy or seen him," says Ken.

"We believe you are Roy Monte due to a trace of evidence in our computer data about an erase of Roy and creation of Ken Carson's profile account just minutes apart," says agent Rodriguez.

"That's absurd," says Ken with a look of disbelief and standing up out of his chair to make his point clear.

Both agent Schmidt and Rodriguez step towards Ken behind his desk. Rodriguez takes Ken by the wrist and quickly cuffs one hand and then the other so that Ken is hand cuffed at the front of his body.

"Roy Monte, you are under arrest for faking your identity. Anything you say can and will be held against you in the court of law . . ." says Agent Schmidt going on to read Roy his rights as agent Rodriguez hand cuffs Roy.

Juan's jaw drops open after noticing Ken leave in hand cuffs, the sucker in his mouth drops to the floor. As the agents escort Roy (Ken) in handcuffs out of the studio, the four employees are frozen still with disbelief.

"Oh no my job, this job, I new it was too good to be true," says Juan putting both hands over his face, spreading fingers apart to see between his fingers, and looking down at the floor.

"The business plan will work, this business is yours now. It will be what you make it, build it and they will come," says Roy just before reaching the door.

*   *   *

Sitting in an interrogation room, Roy is handcuffed and wearing orange jail apparel. The room is fully lit with bright lights and the table surface is bare. His bald head makes the light glare off his forehead.

"Man, Guns N Roses are coming to town, I can't wait to see them live in concert," says agent Rodriguez walking through the door behind agent Schmidt.

"Welcome to the jungle Roy, let's have some fun and games. We'll have everything you want," says Agent Schmidt emulating a Guns N Roses song while raising both arms to forty-five degrees from the shoulder joint.

"Roy, what do you have to say for yourself?" says Agent Rodriguez.

"You caught me, what else can I say?" says Roy.

"This was a good plan Roy, up until evidence in our computer files going back two hundred and fifty years," says Agent Rodriguez scratching his bald forehead and standing behind Roy.

Roy interlaces his fingers together, staring into the dark one sided see through glass in front of him. He winks one eye, smiles, and then says, "Failure is just the beginning."

"Yeah, this failure will be the beginning of some serious jail time," says Agent Schmidt coursing his fingers through his long black hair, looking at his reflection in the one sided window and standing next to Roy.

*   *   *

In the Trenton County Court Room, Roy is seated in the defendants' chair. His long facial hair and bald head of hair make his appearance look unkept with a lack of hygiene. His lawyer, Larry is an older man in his sixties with hair moose parted evenly down the middle and green tie with black vest. The thinly trimmed mustache above his mouth is barely visible.

"All rise, for the final decision," says the judge as everyone in the court room stands.

"Roy Monte, you are found guilty on accounts of faking identity and unlawful business lending practices. You are hereby sentenced to one hundred twenty days in county jail and a fine of fifty grand to your account. A bail of seventy five thousand will be in place," says the brown haired judge before pounding the gavel to signal the court trial conclusion.

Roy looks at his defense lawyer Larry, who's sitting next to him. Looking him in the eyes intently waiting for him to say something, Larry looks down at the table in front of him and decides to break the silence.

"Roy, Exuberant Ways will continue to operate without you, a firm has taken it over with plans to fulfill the original mission statement," says Larry without looking at Roy and snapping his briefcase shut.

"Another failed business venture, how many times will it take to succeed?" says Roy as a police officer attaches his hand cuffs to a set of ankle cuffs.

"First, the business needs to be formed by a real person who actually exists," says Larry as the police officer escorts Roy out of the court room.

CHAPTER 14

Day one hundred and eighteen in Roy's jail sentence is a meager deprivation for Roy. His accounts money grows even more with the fees incurred during his jail time. Sitting in his cell, next to him sits a big bald man with a scar on his forehead stretching diagonally over his left eye.

"Wayne, say Wayne," says Roy trying to get the attention of the person he has been rooming with for over four months.

The jail cell has a fold down cot and a toilet just beneath the sink. Roy's cell has a brick wall with no windows and thick with paint from the multiple coats over the years.

Lying on his cot looking up and hands clasped behind his head, Wayne says, "Where will we be? Where will we be? I must know where we will be when that magnificent day arrives."

"What day is that? What is arriving?" says Roy.

"Oh man, don't you know? The day each of us achieve our higher calling," says Wayne sitting up on his cot to face Roy across the jail cell.

Wayne's eyes and mouth open wide while yawning from the lack of sleep he has been getting. He begins to scratch his lower forearms, which have developed a rash from his many allergies.

"Every human has something no other creature has. This is humans believing in something greater than themselves," says Wayne holding his fists up high.

"My life's work has been to create and help others create. A creation involves working to achieve. That is why I want to provide a way for others to work and create their pursuit to happiness," says Roy walking back and forth, pacing along the cell bars dividing him from Wayne.

"Wayne, Wayne, what is your perception your higher belief? You can bench press four hundred pounds it took six police officers to hand cuff you when you were arrested for burglary," says Roy.

Pausing, Wayne stands and walks towards Roy, which only takes two steps. Cracking the knuckles in his right hand with the left hand, Wayne gives a death defying stare to Roy.

"That belief is in poetry, but my biggest obstacle is trying to get the lines and stanzas right," says Wayne.

Roy almost bursts with laughter but manages to avoid it by giving a chuckle. He backs away from Wayne to be a safer distance from him.

"Poetry is a magnificent creation to believe in. What an impression you can leave the world. Don't let those lines and stanzas trip you. You just have to work with them like a puzzle piece," says Roy.

The inmate across the hall stands up putting his arms through the bars and waving them towards Roy. His small skinny body makes him swim in his prison clothing. A vein is visible on each side of his temple with a black goatee the length of a few inches extending from his chin.

"Look here, we have an Edgar Allen Poe amongst us. Question, what did the Raven quote?" says the man across the hall.

"Bean, put a can in it, don't make me make you eat your green beans again," says Wayne gripping the prison bars in each hand with a serious look on his face.

"Okay, I will notta say anymore, I hate green beans," says Bean looking down in embarrassment at the floor.

"Disregarding the interruption," Wayne says, "You were saying."

"Your creation of poetry is a great calling that defines you," says Roy.

Wayne grabs his chin with his index finger and thumb. Sitting down on his cot, he pauses for a brief moment having arms crossed at his chest. Roy stands still with arms behind his back and hands clasped at waist level.

"If poetry is what defines me, what defines you?" says Wayne.

"The ability to watch things grow, I'm so fascinated by it. Whether it's compound interest for an IRA or a child growing up, I can't get enough of it. With the reversal four decades ago, people are not looking to create, or watch things grow," says Roy shaking his head in disappointment and looking at the ground.

"What are people doing then?" says Wayne.

"They're running inside a revolving door, looking for growth inward instead of outward. It's like an ingrown toe nail, which is the perfect metaphor for trying to reach zero," says Roy sitting on his cot in the prison cell.

*   *   *

Opening up the door to freedom the next day, a bright beam of sun light shines through the prison door exit. Roy is dressed in a casual white t-shirt and black jeans. His tall frame, long brown hair, and facial hair make him look like Abe Lincoln except the top of his head is bald.

Two jail guards escort Roy out of the exit into the parking lot just outside the jail walls. Two armed guards are guarding the exit door at all times with a scout sharp shooter up in the lookout tower. The double bladed barb wire fence is coiled at the top of the prison's stone walls and another strip is coiled on the ground four feet high behind the prison walls. Roy proceeds to walk slowly out of the prison exit.

"Well, you're free," says the prison guard standing to the right of Roy.

"I've seen it, I've seen it with my own two eyes," says Roy with excitement.

"Seen what?" says the jail guard.

"Growth, potential, humungous fortune beyond belief, the ability to create jobs and drive business," says Roy.

"I heard you the other day talking to Wayne. The world you talk of will never exist. How many times will it take to succeed?" says the jail guard.

"Too many people for you to count on your fingers and toes. It is not for everyone, only for those who have the craving and hunger for it," says Roy smiling.

One of the guards looks over to the other guard next to him and says, "I think they shouldn't have let this one go."

"That's what is said about everyone," says the other guard in response.

Roy gets into the back passenger door of the taxi cab waiting in the empty parking lot. The car pauses for a moment, and then drives away leaving a long dust trail behind.

CHAPTER 15

"Hurry up," says Krisa.

Roy wakes up just in time to see the ending of Harry Bathet's speech on military benefits for college students. With Roy's head resting back against the recliner, this makes his hair messy where his hair begins at the back of the head. He quickly pats it down with his fingers but is unable to keep it from sticking back up. As Harry leaves the stage, Roy walks half way to the podium and stops to take a sip of coffee out of his black Don's Coffee mug. His blue dress shirt and kakis stand out with the red stage curtain behind him.

"Thank you Harry, I wish I would have chosen the military after going to college, I regret I didn't serve," says Roy walking to the podium in front of the packed auditorium of six hundred college students.

With beaming lights on Roy, there is applause from the crowd. Roy begins his speech:

"You all here at the U of M are taking part in history. I stand before you today with a plan of action. Over sixty years ago, I made a decision to create a massive amount of wealth that does not exist in today's world and is not what it used to be.

"Look around, everyone is not giving their best for what they believe in. Belief and growth are needed to see the best life has offer not just for our self, but for everyone else. I say we create a movement and bring back capitalism," says Roy pausing.

At first there is silence in the auditorium, and then a distant clapping is heard from the upper back row of the auditorium until slowly more and more people start to clap. Within fifteen seconds most of the auditorium is clapping and some even chanting Roy's name.

"This movement for capitalism is relevant today, we see traces of capitalism still with all you college students looking to gain ground in the job market. If you think that is tough, know this, a capitalistic economy will be easier for you to get the job you aspire. I will be on campus tomorrow morning to relish in the capitalist movement and hope to see you there," says Roy waving then walking off the stage.

*   *   *

The next day there is a protest of students on the steps of the Fine Arts Center University Campus building. Students hold signs reading: "Socialism No More", "Back to Capitalism We Go", and "Wealth Creation = Job Creation".

Roy stands in with the group proudly chanting, "CAPITALISM, CAPITALISM, CAPITALISM!"

Suddenly a loud explosion occurs by the huddled group of protesters, knocking people over and dispersing smoke everywhere. The explosion occurs on the steps next to the hand rail. The steps are part of the entry to the fine arts center where the auditorium is.

"Help, Help!" screams a women as additional screams are heard over and over with people panicking and running for cover.

Campus police are on the scene right away to pull injured victims of the bombing to safety. Roy is still in shock from the blast, he sits at the top steps next to the hand rail. He is the only one from the protest remaining still and has not moved one step since the bombing occurred. A detective approaches from the steps below him.

"Roy Monte, my name is Dustin Wells U of M Campus Security, may I question you about the events that just took place here today?" says Dustin with a tan trench coat and golfing visor.

"Sure, can you get me to calm down first? I don't know how focused I will be as I'm still in shock," says Roy leaning against the weak hand rail moving loosely from the ground post.

* * *

An hour later, Roy is sitting with Dustin at the campus's security office. Dustin's desk is cluttered with stacks of paper files, a desk lamp lights the desk counter top and the left side of his face. Roy sits forward in an attentive manner on the other side of the desk.

"Roy, it is to my knowledge that you started the protest the day before with your speech on capitalism, is this true?" says Dustin with spiked black hair, holding a pen and paper ready to take notes.

"Yes, I was part of the protest and favored the formation of such an action," says Roy giving one head nod.

"Okay, based on this, did you know where the students would protest the following day?" says Dustin quickly asking questions to have Roy respond without much thought.

"Yes, I suggested the location of the protest after my speech yesterday," says Roy.

"During this speech yesterday, were you using a black Don's coffee mug made of plastic?" says Dustin showing his jaw under bite as he talks.

"Yes, it is my favorite coffee mug from my previous business venture, drank a lot of coffee with that mug," says Roy.

Dustin proceeds to make a check mark in his notes and looks up with a smirk on his face. He pauses and makes eye contact with Roy who is now leaning back in his chair. Dustin quickly puts his note paper in a file.

"Great, please let me know if there is anything that comes up related to this incident today. That is all and you are free to go," says Dustin.

Roy stands and leaves the office and is immersed into the evening sunlight when walking out the glass pane front door.

*   *   *

Two days go by after the University bombing and three people are dead with seven injured. Roy sits in the public library researching and prepping his next big speech for capitalism.

Two men and one woman walk into the library and stop next to Roy reading in the chair. All three surround Roy. Roy looks to his sides and rotates to see women standing behind him. The two men are wearing black dress coats and an ear piece in their ear. The woman behind him has black hair in a pony tail and a gray dress coat and pants.

"Are you Roy Monte?" says the woman behind Roy.

"Yes, that would be me," says Roy continuing to read from his book without looking at the agent behind him.

"I'm federal agent Johnson with the FBI, Roy we are going to take you in for some questioning at this time regarding the U of M bombing that occurred earlier this week," says Johnson standing behind Roy.

Roy stands up without grabbing his research materials and leaves the library without any struggle with Johnson and the other two agents. The two men walk on each side of Roy and Johnson walks in front leading the way.

"Just one question, how come you two have ear pieces and she doesn't?" says Roy talking to the big agents walking on both sides of him.

"Agent Johnson doesn't need back up," says the agent to Roy's right.

"What happens when there is back up needed?" says Roy to agent to his right.

The agent to Roy's left responds with a smirk on his face, "We need back up when Agent Johnson decides to let the mayhem begin."

"I see, well I'll be sure not to piss her off," says Roy.

*   *   *

"Do you understand me? We have a photo taken by the press just moments before the bombing showing your black coffee mug in the spot where the bombing took place," says Johnson.

"I don't know what you're talking about; I was not connected in any way to the bombing. That coffee mug in the picture is not mine because I had mine back at hospital room I was staying at," says Roy.

"Whose coffee mug is this if it's not yours? Can a person purchase such a coffee mug today?" says an agent slamming his hand on the table to make everyone jump.

"Roy, this is agent Greenway. He becomes the mean green machine if he doesn't find out the truth behind all of this," says Johnson sitting down across the table from Roy.

Greenway has braided brown hair in corn rows, brown eyes, and no facial hair. He starts to crack the knuckles of his closed fist, flexing his big arm muscles to make his veins stick out. A killer stare in his eyes looks directly at Roy from where he stands across the table.

"Look, I can bring in the Don's Coffee mug that I have to prove it wasn't mine or just hook me up to a lie detector to find out that way," says Roy with high eyebrows and right palm high in the air to suggest he has no information to give the agents.

"Lie detectors are no longer a valid means of discovering the truth," says Johnson tapping her pen against the table edge while sitting back in her chair.

"Will I be tried for this conviction?" says Roy.

"If our lab team can match the piece of the mug to a Don's coffee mug, then you might be convicted," says Johnson.

"We should have the lab results in about a week," says Greenway while standing and leaning forward with both hands resting on the table.

"A week, it took me a week and six business loan applications to start my business at Don's Coffee. Now, how many times will it take to succeed in persuading you? I had nothing to do with the bombing," says Roy in disbelief.

CHAPTER 16

Three months later, Roy sits in the court room at the Minnesota capital, St. Paul. He sits as the defendant with Larry Chanhassen his defense lawyer.

"All rise, this court is now in session, Judge Erickson proceeds," says the court officer at the front of the court floor.

The judge walks in with her black gown loosely draped over her and long brown hair extending down to her shoulders. She sits down and pounds her gavel.

"With court case number 796384 we are now beginning the conviction of Roy Monte in the University of Minnesota bombing on April twenty seventh in the year of two thousand and seventy-two," says Judge Erickson correcting her eye glasses on her face.

"Prosecution, you will go first," says Judge Erickson.

"Your honor, the prosecution will call Gary Braser to the stand," says Sharon the prosecution lawyer.

Walking up to the stand, Braser is a short and stocky man with crew cut brown hair. His loosely fit green dress sweater makes a round upper body look misshapen from the lower body. Standing out of her chair, Sharon goes to the stand where Gary is. Her gray high heels tap loudly when coming in contact with the tile floor. Gary seems relaxed sitting back in his chair and not as intense when Larry was questioning him. A smirk on Gary's face makes it obvious that Sharon and Gary have met before.

Standing before everyone in the court room, Sharon has red hair extending down to her neck with a grey suit and skirt. The crease in her hair line separates her bangs from the rest of her hair.

"How long was Roy standing next to the mug when these pictures were taken?" says Sharon.

"Over fifteen minutes," says Gary.

"How long was Roy standing on the opposite side mug at the top of the steps?" says Sharon.

"About the same, I would say fifteen minutes," says Gary.

"Roy never touched or laid his eyes on this mug that you are of aware of," says Sharon.

"I never seen him look at it or touch it," says Gary.

"No further questions your honor," says Sharon returning to sit at the prosecution table.

"Defense you have an option to question the witness," says Erickson.

The defiant lawyer Larry walks slowly up to the witness stand reading his note pad to himself. Each step he takes has his foot contact the floor heel to toe and pen in hand tapping his thigh repeatedly.

"Gary, you were the journalist taking the pictures of Roy's coffee mug just minutes before the bombing took place, were you not?" says Larry.

"Yes, I took those photos. The last one was five minutes before the bomb going off at 10:05 am," says Gary with obviousness.

"Just because the photo has a Don's Coffee mug is not sufficient evidence linking Roy Monte to the bombing. Don's Coffee shop has been in business for years. Such a mug would be a common sight," says Larry.

"I was there and I seen Roy Monte amongst the protestors. I did not see him holding the black mug, but he stood right next to it for most of the time. In fact, the person to the left of it in the photo is Roy," says Gary leaning forward and talking into the microphone.

"Evidence suggests the bomb was inside this mug, where was Roy when the bomb inside the mug exploded?" says the lawyer preparing to write what Gary says on a writing pad.

"Roy was on the other side of the crowd standing by himself," says Gary.

"That is all your honor," says the defense lawyer Larry to judge Erickson.

"Do you have a witness to put on the witness stand at this time defense?" says judge Erickson.

"We will pass your honor," say Larry.

"Prosecution, you are to go," says Judge Erickson as Gary leaves the witness stand.

Sharon rises and says, "The prosecution calls Roy Monte to the stand."

Roy gets sworn into the stand and sits down with an uncomfortable gesture on his face. His dress shirt and tie are tight fitting and his face is red. Sharon walks up to Roy.

"Roy, did you know the coffee mug was to your left in the photo?" says Sharon.

"No, I never knew there was a coffee mug," says Roy.

"Do you have a coffee mug that says 'Don's Coffee' on it?" says Sharon chewing gum in between her questioning.

"I do, in fact I should still have it in my room at the hospital," says Roy.

Lifting his arm up so that his hand touches his temple, Roy focuses on Sharon's high heel shoes. Staring at the high heels for a few seconds, he squints his eyes, blinks, and looks up as if coming out of a day dream.

"Are there any further questions for the defendant?" says Judge Erickson.

"Yes, Roy, were you under the influence of prescription or over the counter medications during the protest?" says Sharon walking towards the jury.

"I took the generic brand of Vivarin about five hours before the protest," says Roy.

"You were under the influence of this caffeine pill of approximately how many?" says Sharon.

"Two," says Roy.

"Two . . . that is about four hundred milligrams, that's quite the stimulant," says Sharon.

"Have you ever taken a caffeine pill?" says Roy to Sharon.

"That is not a question for me to answer as the prosecution lawyer in this case, you are the person being questioned," says Sharon.

"No, a caffeine pill has no significance to the correlation of the bombing and the horrendous thought of me being the person behind it," says Roy.

"The defendant has a point your honor," says Larry the defense lawyer.

"Please switch the topic under consideration with the defendants questioning Sharon," says Judge Erickson.

"The explosive that was in the mug had to be very compressed and highly charged for something that small to have that much of an explosion, where would someone get materials to make it? Do you know Roy?" says Sharon.

"I wouldn't know where to start with making a bomb," says Roy.

"Did you recently in the past month check out a book at the library called, *The History of Ammunitions and Explosives?*" says Sharon.

"Yes, only because I was interested in the topic from a TV show I recently seen, that's it," says Roy.

"What was the TV show you speak of?" says Sharon.

"The TV show was on the History Channel called, *Bombs: Make, Fuse, and Ignite.* I just wanted to know more about the different types," says Roy leaning forward to speak into the microphone.

Sharon writes down notes in her note pad held in hand and proceeds to the next question with a determined look.

"Your honor, this book called: *Bombs: Make, Fuse, and Ignite* shows how to make bombs. Specifically, there is a Bunker Bomb that is small, having enough force to send out a fifteen foot blast radius as we seen at the campus bombing," says Sharon to Judge Erickson.

"Do you have evidence that Roy checked this book out a month ago?" says Judge Erickson.

"Yes, here is a checkout report from the Trenton library showing Roy had the book for thirteen days," says Sharon handing the report to Judge Erickson.

"Can this Bunker Bomb fit inside a coffee mug? That would be pretty small for a fifteen foot blast radius," says Judge Erickson.

"Yes, it possibly could. I have researched with a military ammunitions specialist by the name of Arnold Vansky. He says a Bunker Bomb is able to fit into a twenty four ounce coffee mug like that used at the campus bombing in this case. Here is the written testimony in his interview," says Sharon handing papers for Judge Erickson to look at.

A long pause occurs as Erickson looks over the interview report. Only the knocking of wood can be heard from a child in the back of the court room, kicking the wooden bench in front of him. Light from a cloudy day beams through the four long vertical windows of the court room, which casts streaks of shadows on the people inside.

"Roy was standing twenty feet from the coffee mug when the bomb went off. With a blast radius of fifteen feet, Roy had no injuries during this event. Any shrapnel would have no harm to Roy with that many people between him and the bomb. Roy, did you purchase a cup of coffee at the Stop n Go convenience store when you stopped in there prior to the protest bombing?" says Sharon.

"Yes," says Roy.

"Was the coffee you bought put into a personal mug?" says Sharon.

"Yes," says Roy.

"What did you do with the mug? Did you bring it with you to the protest?" says Sharon.

"Yes, I did not carry it with me the entire time and put it in my back pack after drinking it all," says Roy.

"In these pictures, of the protest, you do not have a backpack or a mug with you," says Sharon.

"That's because I set it behind the garbage can located on the first platform of the stair entrance," says Roy.

"Didn't you say that your Don's coffee mug was not at the location of the bombing? You said it was at the hospital, in the room you stayed at," says Sharon.

"Yes, I have another mug that is black," says Roy.

"How many more?" says Sharon.

"Over a dozen, I'm not exactly certain," says Roy.

"It is quite clear that the defendant has not told us everything related to the crime scene. We cannot see in the photos a back pack behind the garbage can on the first platform of the stairs. Roy, do you know results of the lab tests on the pieces of the mug at the scene?" says Sharon.

"No," says Roy shaking his head as if he does not want to find out.

"The pieces of the mug at the bombing location were not able to offer any evidence to who did it. However, moments ago Roy Monte lied to the court about the location of his coffee mug during the bombing. In fact, in an interview with campus police and FBI agents Roy said he had no mug at all. No further questions your honor," says Sharon turning around and walking back to take a seat at the prosecution stand.

"Defense, you may proceed," says Judge Erickson looking at Larry.

Larry stands while tightening his tie knot. Walking up to Roy on the stand he takes nothing with him but his folded glasses.

"There is no awareness to you that the mug was sitting on the brick arm rail at the lower base of the stairs to the campus hall," says Larry.

"None," says Roy.

"Tell me everything you did before coming to the protest on April twenty-seventh," says Larry.

"Well, I slept in until seven in the morning from being up all night working on a difficult business plan. I took a shower, shaved, brushed my teeth, and got dressed. Then I listened to the news for forty-five minutes on the Radio. I went and took a couple caffeine pills because I needed to wake up after only getting a few hours of sleep. I went to the Stop N Go Convenience store at about 8: 30 am to fill up with gas and get a mug of coffee. Lastly, I went to the Minnesota Campus for the protest at around nine in the morning," says Roy.

"What did the mug look like and what was its size you filled up with at the convenience store? says Larry.

"It was a black mug I'm not sure what its size was but I know it was bigger than sixteen ounces," says Roy.

"The mug in the bombing photo was black and the one Roy used was black. There is no evidence of any one seeing Roy have contact or awareness of the mug that exploded next to the hand rail. With no forensic evidence, this is a testimony of Roy based on suspicion, that is all your honor," says Larry to everyone in the court.

Standing up, Sharon says, "Objection, the defendant clearly stated that the mug in his back pack was a Don's coffee mug."

"Roy, was the mug in your back pack a Don's coffee mug?" says Judge Erickson.

"No, it was a black coffee mug. I didn't say the mug in my bag was a Don's coffee mug, check the record," says Roy.

The court room officer hands judge Erickson the records of today's court testimony. She flips through the pages of the report and pauses at a page to thoroughly read the testimony more than once.

"Roy is telling the truth, he did not specify any specifics, neither did the questioning specify the in particular, which type of mug it was," says Judge Erickson.

Day one of the trial ends with no direct links between the Don's Coffee mug bombing and Roy.

*   *   *

Day two of the trial occurs on a cloudy day with scattered rain showers outside and a twenty-five mile per hour wind making the rain drop from the sky at an angle. Half way through the trial, the prosecution has its next witness.

"Prosecution you are next for calling a witness," says Judge Erickson after taking a deep breath.

"I call Betty Lynn to the stand," says Sharon wearing dark blue business attire.

A lady of black hair in her thirties stands up in the second row of the court room and walks to the witness stand. She wears blue jeans and a white and purple Nike shirt. Her hair hangs free around her neck on all sides but the front and her bangs extend down to the middle of her forehead.

"Betty, you work at the Stop n Go on 17th Avenue South Trenton, were you working on April 27th when Roy came in?" says Sharon.

"Yes, Roy came in about 8:30 that morning and paid for gas and coffee," says Betty.

"Was he uptight or nervous about anything?" says Sharon.

"He seemed tired and anxious with sleep in his eyes," says Betty shaking her head.

"What did the coffee mug look like, what color was it?" says Sharon.

"The coffee mug was a twenty-four ounce size being black in color," says Betty.

"Do you remember if the mug had writing or a logo on it?" says Sharon.

"It had something, but I don't recall what it was," says Betty squinting her eyes trying to remember what it looked like.

Walking to the prosecution table, Sharon works on her palm computer and turns on the video projector at the front wall of the court room with a remote.

"What I'm about to show the court is a video of Roy at the Stop n Go convenience store on the morning of April 27th . . . . This is Roy and there is Betty behind the store counter," says Sharon pointing with the remote laser on the screen for everyone in the court to see what she is referring to.

"Watch when I freeze it and zoom into the mug," says Sharon freezing the video and zooming into the colored video.

"This mug is black and looks identical to the one in the photo taken at the stairs of the protest shown here," says Sharon pulling up the journalist's photo to get a side by side comparison of the two mugs.

"They even have the same Don's Coffee logo on them and seem to be the same size of twenty-four ounces," says Sharon putting the remote down at her desk and closing her 5 by 8 inch palm computer.

*   *   *

With the decision of the case being announced at the end of the trial day, Judge Erickson takes her position as Judge coming from a break. The jury fills their seats and everyone waits quietly and eager for the decision to be announced.

Judge Erickson pounds her gavel and straightens her glasses on her face as she drinks from a glass of water.

"Roy Monte the jury of this court has unanimously voted you to be found guilty of criminal manslaughter with photographic evidence of the mug being yours in question. Roy's false testimony of the location of his mug has given the jury reason to decide he is guilty. You will serve a prison sentence of three years in jail and will have an acceptable behavior term of thirty-two months. At which time your sentence and the cases evidence will be reviewed and updated," says judge Erickson pounding her gavel.

Roy looks down at his feet in shock that he is being wrongfully convicted of this crime. Dr. Menzel has his left hand over his mouth shaking his head in disbelief, sitting in the second row of the court room audience behind Roy.

"This is not the only shot in succeeding, but keep asking, how many times will it take to succeed?" says Larry clicking his pen shut, tossing it in his suit case, and snapping the latches shut.

Chapter 17

The water drips from the sink about once every three seconds as Roy stares up at the scratch marks on the ceiling of the jail cell. A man moans in pain from a stomach ulcer across from him, which has kept him up for the past day and a half. His three by five foot cot with a three inch thick mattress bottoms out to the metal frame beneath him.

A short jail guard with buzz cut hair slides a plate of food and a cup of water through a doggy door at the bottom of Roy's door. The door is thick with bars and three latches. A second guard passes by the door that is bald, wearing a black uniform, and is in his late forties.

"Lunch time, it's left over meat loaf your favorite. Everyone sure is quiet today, is it me or is someone in a bad mood?" says the second guard chuckling with laughter.

The finger food meal consists of a slice of meat loaf, a bun, and a cob of corn. When done, Roy slides his meal tray next to the doggy door for the guard to pick up.

"Recess time," says the same guard arriving at Roy's door with one other guard being younger and bigger in height.

Roy gets escorted to an area the size of a basketball court with other inmates for afternoon time out of cell lasting thirty minutes. There are fifteen other inmates there, some socializing while standing in a circle and other groups playing games of dice.

"Hey my name is Brad Beasley, been here for two years for a burglary I didn't do," says a man with thick facial hair, brown curly hair, dried out skin, and tattoos of dragons on his arms.

"Brad, my name is Roy, I'm also wrongly accused for a bombing and have been here a few weeks. Can't seem to come to terms with what I'm going to do when I get out of here. As the world has changed so much with my values being split in two," says Roy standing and crossing his arms at his chest.

"A person's values are something they will always have no matter what happens. In fact, the value of freedom has supposedly been taken from me in jail. I think other wise, due to the fact I still am free to think my own thoughts and control my own actions. Even while in jail I can choose to think of freedom as being in my possession," says Brad interlocking his fingers together and stretching his arms overhead.

"Perhaps, I will take that into consideration when searching for relief in my confined prison cell, thanks," says Roy pulling his orange prison pants up with the waist being about two sizes too big.

*   *   *

Roy's hand shakes from having low blood sugar and his stomach growls with hunger. The prison guard comes to collect the plate of food being refused to eat.

"Nothing again, I don't know why a person would fast while serving a sentence in jail," says the guard grabbing the tray and staring at Roy sitting down on his cot across the cell.

"Having control is freedom," says Roy to the guard.

"Choosing to not eat is depriving to me not freedom, suit your self dude," says the guard walking away.

Agitated with discomfort, Roy shakes his head from the confusion of not being able to make sense of his next step in life. The inmate with the stomach ulcer across the hall talks to himself as if someone is right next to him, but there is no one.

"Where is your favorite place to eat on Friday nights? I bet you've never been to a drive in café with a signature cheeseburger and curly fries. Curly fries, waffle fries, straight cut fries, potato wedges, tater tots, what do you like? I like my curly fries," says the unknown inmate with a stomach ulcer.

*   *   *

A couple of guards stand in front of Roy's cell, one carries hand cuffs and ankle shackles the other guard holds a night stick tucked in his arm pit.

"Roy, you got company, Larry is here to see you," says the guard unlocking his prison cell door.

Roy stands as one guard cuffs and shackles his limbs while the other stares at Roy with caution to his every movement. The guard's metal baton held with one hand is sure to put a beating on even the biggest man. The two guards and Roy walk to the visitor booth where Larry is.

Roy sits down and lifts up his phone to talk to Larry seated on the other side of the protective window. Larry is wearing a business suit with a black tie.

"Roy, I got great news, they might let you off early," says Larry.

"Yes, that's what I'm talking about," says Roy.

"It's about time we get you out of here, but in order to get out of here, we must first know how we got in here," says Larry.

"What do you mean, I'm innocent until proven guilty and that hasn't happened," says Roy with disbelief in response to what Larry says.

"Looking back, we kind of brought this jail sentence on ourselves by falsely telling the total truth and switching the testimony about the mug you carried with you during the bombing. A change of testimony did not persuade the jury in our favor," says Larry looking overwhelmed and taking his glasses off to rub his tired eyes with his fingers.

"They should have reiterated their understanding so I could correct them. A misunderstanding should not be a false testimony," says Roy shaking his head.

"Enough with the blame, I'm here to get you out of here. This is all we should be focusing on right now," says Larry pointing his index finger down on the table to show the importance about getting to the point.

Roy hangs up the phone on the receiver with a look of disgust on his face. He looks into Larry's eyes for a long time to test his nerves to see if he is hiding any intentions. Larry smiles and points to Roy's phone on the receiver by angling his index finger in front of the glass window.

Roy picks up the phone and says, "You know I'm getting out soon otherwise you wouldn't have come here. You wouldn't bring bad news."

"You get out tomorrow Roy," says Larry.

"Yes!" says Roy his left fingers snap three times and looks up to the ceiling being grateful.

"You will have some restrictions with probation and a weekly check in by a probation officer," says Larry.

Roy hangs up the phone on the receiver and gives Larry a standing salute to show some foolishness. Once Roy has left the room, Larry slides his notebook in his book bag and carries it on his right shoulder. He walks away leaving the phone resting on the booths table without hanging it on the receiver.

Getting out of jail in the thirty-two month revisionary period of the court system is a path to a new life for Roy. Not finding enough evidence in his false conviction requires no further punishment by the rules of the judicial system.

Roy takes a cab back to Trenton, Minnesota where he resides at Dr. Menzel's house for the time being.

The house has a three stall garage connected to it with a large dining room with a sun roof. A bar table separates the dining room from the kitchen and a large hallway goes down to individual bedrooms, guest rooms, offices, and libraries. The hall way must have at least ten rooms total on each side.

The chandelier in the dining room has spiraling lights that extend down to the lengthy dining table. Two big patio windows look to great views outside, one to the front lawn, the other to the back yard where there is a big pool.

"Dr. Menzel, are you good at writing press releases?" says Roy with a green Nike sweatshirt that says "Just Do It." on the front.

"Never in all my years, I have submitted some research at the hospital to a medical journal but never to a magazine or newspaper," says Dr. Menzel standing and leaning forward onto the bar table looking ahead at Roy standing in the dining room.

"I want to get word out about society's need or a person's need to choose what happens to them and deciding for themselves how much they can earn with the old free enterprise system," says Roy.

"There aren't too many people trying to be separate from the government like that, Roy," says Dr. Menzel.

"I'm going to create a blog, just a discussion on the internet about my vision of a free enterprise system. I will write this," says Roy taking a folded piece of paper out of his pocket and handing it to Dr, Menzel for review:

> I believe in a day where a free enterprise system will produce plentiful lives for those producing most influential products/services. Intrinsically working for a life of enrichment will have a contagious effect on everyone. In a current system where working people consume less to eliminate debt only deprives people of the venture of seeking a cause greater than them selves. Slapping regulations on a free enterprise system is a control device for becoming too big, accruing debt, and living a lifestyle beyond personal means. Have fewer regulations in place to allow people to spend what they want to spend to give the message of: "help me help you". Customers will get what they want, businesses will earn a profit, and the government will get its tax money. Join me on this day to conduct a pursuit of capitalism with a two week fast. Let this fast symbolize our commitment and bond in

pursuing a society where hard work pays off
when trying to achieve your dreams.—Roy

Dr. Menzel looks it over and suggests, "Go through with this Roy, but know this. The government will not like this if U.S. Officials find this, we as citizens have a freedom of speech. However, people have tried to return to a capitalistic society with no success."

Roy goes directly to Dr. Menzel's palm computer sitting on the dining table to submit his blog on his personal webpage. He also submits the blog to two other blog sites. The computer consists of a small three by five inch device that projects a screen into the air above and a foldable keyboard made of plastic with tiny wire chips inside.

Within minutes after posting the blog, Roy gets his first response:

> I agree with you about working for reward. The government has regulated everything with cracking down on debt and living beyond personal means. The reversal theory does make people live in their means and acquire less debt, but the advancements of hard working people are less common today. Reward should be the result of work, instead of work resulting in being able to get by in mediocrity. –Yyamar

Six minutes later, the second one posts:

> Great, when do we start?—Shanan

Today—Roy replies

*   *   *

In a week's time, Roy has over three hundred responses to his blog with everyone except one person wanting to join the two week fast. Roy checks the blog daily to see how things are progressing and responds to the blogs that catch his eye.

Roy and Dr. Menzel sit on a leather couch watching TV at the doctor's house. The entertainment room they are in is enormous with a big screen being projected on the wall. The news is on and more conflict about the mechanized war between China and Australia is on. The war has lasted nine months and so far no human casualties with unmanned air assault machines doing most of the fighting. Downed aircraft is three hundred fifty for China and four hundred twelve for Australia.

"Keep creating more blogs Roy, spread the word," says Dr. Menzel multitasking texting on his phone, watching TV, and talking to Roy.

"I've been reading how Mahatma Gandhi used to fast and I don't know he did it. He went almost three weeks and I'm having a hard time doing a week right now," says Roy.

"You've been living and breathing this capitalistic movement with a lot of dedication Roy. How many hours would you say you have so far?" says Dr. Menzel stopping the multitasking by looking at Roy and putting his phone in his pocket.

"Yeah, I haven't been keeping track, I hope this follows through with a march on Washington. I guess if I fail, I will conclude that I've learned more from not getting what I want than getting what I want," says Roy flipping the channel to a reality T.V. show called *Against All Odds*.

"You will do fine Roy. Just ask yourself, are you able to see through the task at hand? Are you able to see past it? How about around it? The light at the end of the tunnel, do you see it? Is it beyond your reach? Go for it, go after it, it's yours, you own it, take it!" says Dr. Menzel clenching fist and raising his left arm in the air.

"Yeah, that's what I'm talking about," says Roy standing up off the couch, jumping up and down with both arms overhead and fists clenched.

"Just like this T.V. show *Against All Odds*, humans can truly do miraculous things," says Roy daydreaming into the clear T.V. projection on the wall.

*   *   *

Day thirteen arrives and Roy is almost falling asleep with little energy and a bottle of water at his side to stay hydrated. Having his body feed off itself creates toxic ketones in the body making him uncomfortable. Sitting on the couch at Dr. Menzel's house, there are over twenty thousand bloggers responding to his original blog. Roy posts his next blog:

> To all aspiring capitalists, I now call into action a march at the Washington Monument where we will stand at the capital and protest for a free enterprise economic system. With our presence and freedom of speech, congress will know what we value and what most of America aspires to have. I don't know about you, but I like to see things grow and not balance out to remain at zero or be stagnant. Let our vision of capitalism ignite and spread like wild fire.

Dr. Menzel enters the living room and sits down next Roy on the couch. Wearing his red work tie, he lifts it out of the way from being folded into his body when sitting. He carries a tall glass of drink in his right hand.

"What's going on Roy?" says Dr. Menzel taking a sip of his iced drink.

"Just posted a blog to rally everyone to march on Washington," says Roy with raised eyebrows and eyes looking at the computer screen.

"Oh, all in, is this attempt number three? How many times does it take to succeed?" says Dr. Menzel.

CHAPTER 18

The sunny day at the Washington Monument has no clouds in the sky. It's eight in the morning and Roy is setting up the speakers for his speech at the steps of the Washington Monument. Already, participants from the blog are there sitting in lawn chairs and sitting in the grass. One person in a construction worker outfit with a hard hat waves a sign reading, "Work to gain money not to lose money".

"Testing, testing one two," says Roy trying out the microphone to see if it works.

"Over there in the hard hat, I like your sign. What's your name?" says Roy over the speaker.

"Dusty," says Dusty.

Roy switches to the other side of the crowd and points to a blond sitting on a blanket wearing a blue USA shirt. The woman is focusing her attention on Dusty.

"How about you, what is your name and where are you from?" says Roy.

"Names Tina and I'm from Nashville, Tennessee," says Tina in the blue USA shirt.

"Wow, all the way from Nashville, what made you come this far because I have to know?" says Roy.

"I lost my business two years ago due to not being able to generate enough income as a parent with three kids," says Tina shouting and cupping her hands around her mouth so Roy can hear her fifty feet away.

"I wish I had your energy Tina," says Roy before shutting off the loud speaker.

A teenage boy approaches Roy standing behind the podium, looking up to him in his business attire. The adolescent wears Nike Basketball shoes, red shorts, and an Under Armor shirt with the logo displayed in the middle of the shirt. His curly blond hair and blue eyes shine and reflect off the suns brightness.

"Sir, you are very high up right now, how did you get to be so smart," says the boy.

"What's your name?" says Roy taking a seat at the top step next to the boy.

"Jimmy," says the boy named Jimmy.

"Jimmy come on now, are you kidding? You think I'm smart? Really I'm not smart at all. I had to work twice as hard as everyone else to get what I want. I think I'm a delivery driver traveling through hell sometimes because that is what I end up going through to get what I want. I go through hell and come back with what I want," says Roy squinting his eyes with a smirk on his face.

Jimmy looks dumb founded and surprised by what Roy has just said. Roy pauses to let Jimmy think while looking down the steps.

"How old are you Jimmy?" says Roy.

"Thirteen sir," says Jimmy.

"Belief is a powerful value to those who never let go of it. What do you want to be when you grow up?" says Roy.

"A police officer," says Jimmy with a wide smile.

"Your belief will get you there to become one, and perhaps police commissioner to the entire city. Now, wouldn't that be something?"

Jimmy walks down the steps in awe over his talk with Roy. By a quarter to noon an enormous crowd has gathered at the steps of the Washington Monument with at least twenty thousand people present. The sun beams directly from above allowing little shade for all the people standing and crowded together.

Roy walks up to the podium on top of the steps and waves to everyone saying, "Hi, hello everyone, I have a visionary dream."

Suddenly, Roy is hit with a single gun shot and falls over to the right of the podium on the ground. Lying motionless, members of the crowd start to panic and scream. The crowd scatters and slowly calms down upon realizing that it is an assassination.

"I have no pulse, he's probably not going to make it," says a paramedic in white t-shirt and black pants.

The paramedics work on Roy. He is later pronounced dead at the scene and taken off in a black body bag.

Come evening the sign saying "Work to save money, not to lose money" is on a wooden lathe poked in the ground standing up and facing the steps of Washington Monument.

*   *   *

Ten years later, Krisa is at a local bar playing pool with a couple of friends. The game is tied three solid balls to three striped balls, with Krisa playing against a tall woman in a black tank top and silk shorts.

With diamond earrings in both ears, Krisa has her hair dyed black covered by a red bandana. Her blue jeans and a red Harley Davidson shirt fit perfectly to her toned and curvy body. She finishes a behind the back shot across the table to the far corner. Going again after making the shot, she attempts to angle the seven striped ball into a side pocket and misses.

"You're up Barb," says Krisa shaking her head.

"Perfect, you are going to lose now," says Barb rolling the pool stick in between her hands, focusing her eyes on the pool table.

Barb hits in a two solid and four solid ball to the same corner by bouncing the white ball back to realign with a solid ball shot to the same corner. Now, the solid white ball stays in the corner and she chalks the end of her pool stick while studying the pool table.

"I like this corner! Keep the good times a rolling," says Barb calling her shot and walking around the pool table to study different shot angles.

Krisa looks on with a girl watching the run Barb is displaying. The girl wears black snake skin boots, blue jeans, a white t-shirt and cowboy hat.

"Wear did you learn to shoot Barb?" says the girl in the white cowboy hat.

"Growing up we had a pool table in the basement, we used to play every evening after dinner Kate," says Barb stepping towards the table for her next shot attempt.

Barb smacks the white ball hard with a crack and angles the last solid ball into a corner pocket. The eight ball is all that is remaining. When the pool table becomes motionless for the final shot, the white ball is not in a good location. The striped ball is in between the white balls path to the black eight ball.

"The best part about a game of pool is you must propose the shot in order to execute it," says Barb drawing her pool stick back, taking the shot, and bouncing the white ball off the side wall. Upon ricocheting off the side wall, the eight ball is smacked into the opposite side pocket. After the white ball hits the eight ball, it stops and spins in place showing an intended signature ending by Barbara.

"That's game," says Kate.

In the back corner where the restroom is located, a TV is turned on to the evening news. The news anchor announces the evening's headlines: "This just in, congress has just passed a law to switch the economic system to a free enterprise system. The regulations will be in effect similar to where they are now so that a world economic debt crisis does not occur similar to over eighty years ago."

The station switches to a live press conference interview in Washington of the president saying, "These changes will eliminate the reversal theory and bring back capitalism to the world so that great efforts can produce great rewarding achievements for those willing to do it."

Looking at the TV, Krisa says with a smile, "You've got it Roy, take it all the way."

Pausing in deep thought, Krisa arranges the pool table for another game. She shuffles the solid and striped balls around in the triangular template.

"How many times does it take to succeed?" says Barbara with a zipped lip smile.

"Well, beyond the first thought of quitting with a decision to keep trying, no matter the consequences. It's for better or for worse," says Krisa smacking the white ball into the triangular group of balls for the opening break.